Dark Sunshine looked o[...] filly's slender, black legs kicked and her tiny body bucked on its side.

The books said the foal might try to stand in ten minutes. This time, the books were wrong.

The just-born filly was already struggling to stand up.

Now Sam could see her whole body. She had a tiny dished face and huge, luminous eyes. She was satiny black without a speck of white.

Sam realized one of her rubber-gloved hands was pressed against her chest, but her heart had already gone out to the filly.

She'd never seen anything so wonderful. So beautiful.

Only once.

And then Sam remembered.

The tiny black filly looked just like her father.

Read all the books about the

Phantom Stallion

Phantom Stallion

∾ 12 ∾
Rain Dance

TERRI FARLEY

AVON BOOKS

An Imprint of HarperCollinsPublishers

Library of Congress Catalog Card Number:
2003097421
ISBN 0-06-058313-4

First Avon edition, 2004

AVON TRADEMARK REG. U.S. PAT. OFF. AND IN OTHER COUNTRIES,
MARCA REGISTRADA, HECHO EN U.S.A.

Visit us on the World Wide Web!
www.harperchildrens.com

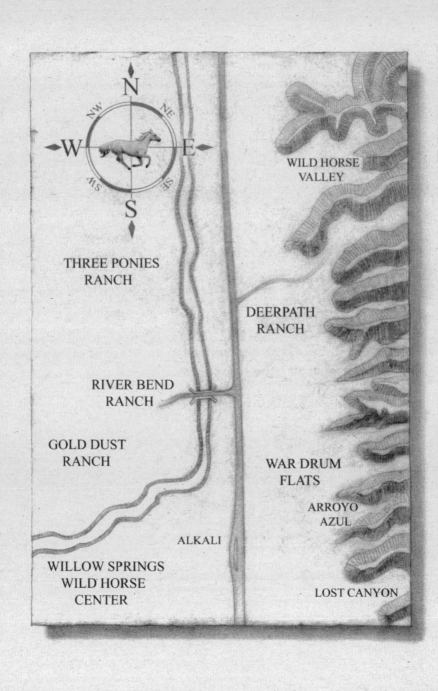

Chapter One ↬

"Happy birthday to me," Samantha Forster sang as she swept the last bit of straw from the big box stall. "Happy birthday to me. . . ."

She set the broom aside with a sigh and picked up the tool Dad had designated a floor scraper.

Summer vacation had started yesterday, today was her birthday, and what was she doing? Working harder than she would have been at school, that was for sure. Even in P.E. she didn't sweat like this.

Not that she felt sorry for herself.

Gram was in the kitchen preparing tonight's birthday dinner, to which Jake and Jen, her best friends, were invited. There would definitely be presents and curiosity was fizzing inside her.

No, she didn't feel sorry for herself, just sort of disgruntled. And it was all her stepmother's fault. Brynna was to blame.

Sam wiped her brow with the back of her wrist. The stall looked cleaner than it ever had, but for Dark Sunshine to foal here, it must be spotless. Sam kneeled and kept working. She'd do anything for the horses of River Bend Ranch.

Or any horses, she thought, as she chipped at a stubborn clump of dirt. But she was giving this chore special care because this stall would be the birthplace of the Phantom's foal.

Luckily, Dad and Dallas, the ranch foreman, had done the hard part by adding wooden partitions to her calf Buddy's open stall to create a place perfect for foaling.

It had only been empty for a few days. After she'd turned Buddy free to live with the other cattle, a sweet yellow calf she'd named Daisy had lived in the stall.

But then Daisy had gotten a new mother.

In late spring, new colts and calves were all over the range, but one young cow wearing a River Bend brand had given birth to a stillborn calf. Seeing this, Dad had galloped back to the ranch, gathered up Daisy, and taken her to the confused cow, who'd adopted Daisy at once.

It was the happiest possible ending, Sam told herself.

She would have been satisfied and happy if Brynna

hadn't been forcing her to make an impossible decision.

She could either go on the annual spring cattle drive—where she'd ride all day, eat wonderful chuck wagon meals, listen to stories around the campfire, and sleep under the stars—or stay home and keep Dark Sunshine company as she gave birth.

A clamor of neighs came from outside, underlining the fact that everyone was going on the cattle drive first thing the next morning. Dad and the cowboys were loading horses, getting ready to truck them out onto the range. She'd already hugged Ace, her frisky bay gelding, good-bye. He was a top cow horse and he'd go on the drive without her if she decided to stay with Dark Sunshine.

Sam stood and wiped her palms on her jeans. The stall floor looked cleaner than her bedroom carpet. The chore hadn't taken that long. She had time to exercise Dark Sunshine before the day got any hotter.

Sam ducked into the tack room and grabbed Sunny's green nylon halter. As she came out, she heard footsteps approaching. They must be Gram's, since Brynna was at work at Willow Springs Wild Horse Center and the sound of tires clunking over the bridge said Dad and the cowboys had left with most of the horses.

Sam waited, eager to take credit for her hard work.

"My, my," Gram said, hands on the hips of her denim skirt as she stood silhouetted in the barn door. "Never thought I'd see the day Wyatt would go to such trouble for a mustang."

Sam loved wild horses, so Gram's words grated, but they were true.

Above all, Dad was a cattleman. He resented anything that threatened or competed with his red and white Hereford cattle. That included wild horses, which sometimes grazed on the same grass the cows needed to eat.

Dad admitted wild horses could be smart and beautiful, even useful once they'd been trained to saddle. But cattle earned the money to keep River Bend Ranch running. They came first.

"And it's nice and clean, isn't it?" Sam nudged her Gram for a compliment.

"Sure is," Gram said as she touched the barn wall, noticing Dad had filled the gaps between boards, so there wouldn't be breezes to chill the new foal. "Look at that overhead lighting. We'll be able to watch the mare every minute." Gram glanced up at the fluorescent lights among the rafters. "And Brynna's supposed to bring a load of wheat straw for bedding tonight, isn't she?"

Sam admitted she was. The best thing about her stepmother was that she loved wild horses, too.

"All for a mustang." Gram shook her head in amazement.

Sam didn't say it, but she was pretty sure Dad had done all this work for her, too.

Hoping it was a sign of good things to come, she crossed her fingers, then her thumbs. Though Dad hadn't promised, she thought he'd let her keep this foal to replace Blackie, the colt who'd run away to become the Phantom.

But what if Dad had done all this work for Brynna?

"What is causing that frown?" Gram asked, rubbing a finger between Sam's eyebrows.

Sam couldn't help smiling. Gram had the magic touch. Not only that, her hand smelled like pie dough. Instead of a birthday cake, Sam had asked for a strawberry pie and Gram had made it with the tiny red garden berries she'd been guarding from the robins.

"I'd think you'd be a pretty happy girl today," Gram said, not quite scolding.

"I am," Sam said, but when Gram raised her eyebrows, she added, "Gram, I don't know why Brynna can't just go along with my plan."

"Well, honey," Gram began, trying to hide her smile, "I imagine she doesn't want to. It's always surprising, isn't it, when people turn out to have minds of their own?"

Sam grumbled as she walked, almost in step, with Gram. The level stretch of dirt glared white in the midday sun. From the barn, it reached to the ranch house, with the ten-acre pasture on one side and the barn corral and round pen on the other.

"But it's the perfect solution," Sam protested. "Brynna's going to work every day anyway. She could just pick me up wherever we made camp each evening, then drive me home to the ranch. Dad says most mares foal at night, so I could sleep in the barn and be with Dark Sunshine. Then, on her way to work in the morning, Brynna could just drop me off again."

"She wants to join the drive after work," Gram pointed out. "She's never been on a cattle drive and neither has Penny. Admit it, dear, if Penny were yours, you'd want to see how she did on the trail."

Sam gave a grudging nod. Brynna's blind mustang mare was well schooled and willing. She followed her rider's cues instantly. It would be fascinating to see if she responded as well amid the distractions of a cattle drive.

"Now that she's part of the family," Gram went on, "Brynna wants to be part of the fun, too."

"Maybe she can't have everything," Sam muttered.

"I think that's her point," Gram said.

It was totally clear to Sam that, as usual, the one who didn't get what she wanted was *her*.

Sam set her jaw and considered not speaking to Brynna when she got home tonight. Maybe that would bring her around.

"Samantha, this is just a tempest in a teapot. Let it go," Gram said.

"I'm not even sure what that means," Sam admitted, hands on her hips.

"A tempest is a storm, dear. The saying sort of means lots of noise and excitement in one little place or, in this case, on one day. This time next year, you won't remember how mad Brynna made you," Gram said, shaking her head.

Gram might be right. She usually was. But if Brynna would just go along with her plan, things would be much easier.

"We don't need another stubborn person in this family," Sam insisted, and this time Gram didn't try to hide her amusement. She laughed out loud.

Sam's path parted from Gram's as she walked toward the ten-acre corral. All but four horses had been trucked away, and three of those left behind neighed frantically and rushed from fence to fence in the open pasture.

Popcorn, the albino mustang, seemed the most agitated, but the two older horses, Amigo and Sweetheart, were alarmed, too. Even tame horses depended on their herd for security. When their herd was split up, they feared the change meant trouble.

Only one of the pastured horses wasn't running. The buckskin tossed her head, swinging her glossy black mane and forelock in agitation, but Dark Sunshine didn't run.

Heavy with foal, she leaned against the fence,

resting one tawny hip there to take some weight off her slender, black-shaded legs.

According to the vet, Sunny had gained over a hundred pounds. Her delicate, dished head looked out of proportion to her belly. Sam hoped the foal's birth date was near.

Sam opened the pasture gate and slipped inside. Amigo and Sweetheart rushed to her. Popcorn followed a few steps behind. All of them snuffled with flared nostrils, checking to see if Sam was carrying grain. When they discovered she wasn't, they backed away, eyes rolling wildly as if only food could have taken their minds off their missing friends.

"Sorry to let you down," she said, and kept walking.

At first, Dark Sunshine watched her approach, then swiveled her head and pricked her ears toward the Calico Mountains.

The buckskin stared, unblinking, then stamped once. She listened intently, as if she heard wild horses calling.

Sam clucked at the mare. Sunny turned one ear in Sam's direction, but her attention stayed on the mountains.

Sam scuffed her boot on the dirt, but the mare did nothing. Sam lifted the halter so that the buckle jingled and finally she had the mare's attention.

"We've got to work together on this, Sunny." Sam kept walking as she talked to the buckskin.

"You've been here almost a year. The Phantom—" Sam bit her lip.

Even though Sunny wouldn't understand, she couldn't bring herself to tell the mare that the stallion had probably forgotten her.

Sam stopped a few steps from the mare. She stood close enough to touch her, but she only waggled the halter and lead rope again.

Sunny raised her head and focused her serious brown eyes on Sam.

"There's a lot better chance of keeping your baby right here, where you can watch him grow up, if he's sweet and tame." Holding her breath, Sam placed her hand flat on the mare's shoulder.

The mare tolerated the touch without twitching her skin or shrinking away. That was good. Even though she'd worked with the mare almost every day, Sam still wasn't sure how the buckskin felt.

She knew how Ace felt. He considered her a kindly boss, who made his life easier with food and shade, but made him work for it. Once in a while, though, when she treated him as a pet, Ace treated her as his simpleminded friend. That's when he forgot how to be ground-tied or surprised her with a buck.

The Phantom considered her his equal. She'd never tell anyone that, especially Jake or Dad. Both insisted only a fool would allow a dangerous animal to think for himself instead of being ruled by humans.

"But you, Sunny," she crooned to the mare, "have

no bad habits whatsoever. So you can't possibly teach your baby to misbehave, right?"

With the halter buckle in her left hand and the green strap in her right, Sam slipped the noseband on the mare. She swung the loose end over the far side of Sunny's head, behind her ears, and buckled the halter snugly.

Sam let out her breath in a rush, but she didn't feel satisfied.

Sunny's attention was still focused on the far mountains. Did she sense it was the time of year the Phantom would need a lead mare?

Even Sam didn't know if the stallion was still ruling his herd alone.

Queen, the red dun who'd guided his herd, had been injured and taken off the range for her own protection. A second mare who'd bid for the top position had died when she'd drunk water tainted with naturally occurring poison.

Star, the pinto mare Jake had caught, gentled then set free on tribal lands, seemed too young for the job, but Sam had seen them running together once.

In summer, when wild stallions tried to build up their harems by stealing from other bands, lead mares were vital. They searched out good grazing and took command of the herd when the stallions were in battle.

But Dark Sunshine couldn't be the Phantom's lead mare. Not only did she wear a BLM brand, but in a few weeks she'd become part of the Horse and Rider Protection program.

HARP helped mustangs that had been adopted by people who had failed at gentling and training them. When those mistakes damaged the horses, HARP took the mustangs back and matched them with at-risk girls. Together, the girls and horses started over.

Last summer, River Bend Ranch had piloted the HARP program for northern Nevada. Though Sam had been dubious at first, HARP had worked well for Popcorn and Mikki, the former runaway who'd been paired with him.

Sunny had been too traumatized by her first owners to be part of the HARP program then, but this summer, Sam hoped the mare would benefit from it.

"Don't keep looking up there, girl," Sam chided the mare, but she didn't explain that the worst thing that could happen would be if Dark Sunshine escaped, only to be recaptured. It would be awful if she lost her freedom twice.

Sam jiggled the lead rope. Sunny shook her head as if wakened from sleep. Then, she lowered her head and nudged Sam's shoulder affectionately.

It wasn't much, but it made Sam grin.

"All right. That's better. Let's go for a walk, pretty girl."

As they left the pasture, a fresh breeze cooled

them both and Sunny turned her attention from the mountains. She clopped beside Sam, keeping an eye on Blaze, the ranch dog that sat on the front porch. She watched the fluttering sleeve of a sweatshirt Sam had draped over the hitching rail earlier in the day, too, but she seemed alert for something else.

Suddenly a faint neigh came from far away. This time Sam heard it, too.

Chapter Two ∾

Chills rained down Sam's neck and arms, but she tightened her grip on the lead rope.

As Sunny answered the neigh, her body vibrated and her weight shifted between her front hooves.

It couldn't be him, Sam thought.

Sunny pawed three times, and dirt pelted Sam's jeans. She braced her legs apart, standing firm in case the mare bolted. She'd seen too many horses break loose and run for the range not to be prepared.

"Sunny. Sunny girl."

The mare's ears pointed toward La Charla and the wild side of the river.

"You can't go back, girl," Sam told the mare. "Just let yourself be happy here, okay?"

An engine roared from the highway. It slowed and downshifted. Sam didn't recognize it by sound and it was a bad time to be distracted.

So, instead of standing on tiptoe to see, Sam walked in the opposite direction.

"Let's check out your new pasture," she invited Sunny.

The small pasture off the barn had been double-fenced for safety. Dad had stapled wire mesh over the wooden rails. The mesh went down to the ground so not even the tiniest, most determined foal could scoot underneath and get in trouble.

"We're moving you over here tonight, Sunny. Won't this be great?"

The mare wasn't listening to her. She was distracted by the sound of the approaching vehicle. Sam hoped it wasn't Mrs. Allen, who drove like a crazy woman, or Linc Slocum, who thought about nothing but himself.

Slow down, Sam ordered herself. *Walk*. Every pulse of worry would telegraph up the halter rope to the mustang's sensitive head.

Against her will, Sam imagined Dark Sunshine scared and rearing. What if she wrenched her neck, or slipped and fell? With only days until she was due to foal, Sunny couldn't be allowed to panic and struggle. It could endanger her baby.

Stop it, Sam ordered herself. There was no reason to be so paranoid. She chanced a quick glance back and noticed Blaze scratching frantically at the front door, begging Gram to let him in.

Sam sighed in relief. There was only one visitor Blaze tried to avoid.

Dr. Scott, the veterinarian, wasn't due to give Sunny her checkup until that afternoon. But apparently he'd arrived early.

The vet's truck bumped over the River Bend bridge, confirming her guess.

"Hey, Sam," he called from his truck.

Dressed in jeans and a dirt-smeared blue-and-white-checked shirt, Dr. Scott climbed out. Watching Sunny, he closed his truck door gently, then sauntered toward them.

Dr. Glen Scott was a young, blond veterinarian. He wore black-rimmed glasses and a smile. A hard-working bachelor, he was always hungry, and Gram loved to feed him.

It was almost lunchtime. Sam wondered if that was why he was early, until he explained.

"Don't know if it's the humidity or what," Dr. Scott said, "but I've had more crazy animals this morning. Some people who were just traveling through on their way to California stopped with a cat who'd been yowling for over two hundred miles. Nothing was wrong, but since Kitty didn't seem to be enjoying the drive, I gave her something to calm her nerves. Then your friend Jen called—"

"Oh no!" Sam said.

"Again, no big deal," Dr. Scott soothed her. "Just that new palomino Rose decided to get her head stuck while reaching for a few extra oats from the feed room. Jed needed some help and no one was tall enough except Slocum, and he was no help at all, so they called me. Since I was in the neighborhood, I decided to pay your mama-to-be a visit."

"Thanks," Sam said. She noticed he still stood a few yards away, giving Sunny time to get used to his presence.

Dr. Scott had only been a vet for two years, but Brynna had been so impressed with his emergency work at the rodeo, she'd hired him to oversee the health of the mustangs at the Willow Springs holding corrals.

"How's she doing?" Dr. Scott asked. "Notice any changes?"

"She's hungry all the time," Sam said. "And I think she's worn out from carrying that baby around. Still, even when she looks too tired to eat, she keeps grazing. Gram's been cooking up bran mash with carrots like you suggested."

"She'll need all those calories—for the birth and for feeding her foal. How's her temperament? Since you're the closest thing she's got to a friend, you're the best judge."

"She's less sociable with the other horses. She wants them around, but she hasn't been standing head to tail with Popcorn, swishing flies, like she did before. I think it hurts his feelings. Not that she's cranky," Sam added, "just sort of distracted."

"Eleven months of pregnancy seems like forever to her, too. But she's nearly finished. Can you get her to come a little closer?"

Sam clucked to the mare and started forward.

For the first time, the mare took a good look at Dr. Scott. With a startled squeal, she jerked back on the rope.

Sam felt ligaments stretch to hold her arms in her shoulder sockets. She braced her legs to keep Sunny from pulling her off her feet.

"She remembers me," the vet said. His lips twisted in a way that said he wished she weren't scared, so Sam didn't mention that Blaze had tried to escape, too.

Both animals remembered their shots better than they did Dr. Scott's kindness.

"You okay?" the vet asked as Sam rolled her shoulders, trying to loosen the muscles after the sudden jerk.

"Sure," Sam answered.

When Dr. Scott just nodded, Sam grinned. If Dad or Jake had been watching, they would have fretted, then tried to take over.

"C'mon, girl." Sam clucked to calm the mare. "No shots today."

As if she understood, Sunny relaxed, standing with one hind hoof cocked. Taking that as permission, Dr. Scott crooned and ran his hands over the mare, paying special attention to Sunny's udder.

"She's getting plenty of milk for the foal. That means we're really close." The vet glanced toward the small pasture near the barn, but his hands kept smoothing Sunny's coat. "You got all the weeds pulled, looks like. I hope you didn't find any fescue?"

"Not a bit," Sam said. "And we all looked."

Dad had taught her to recognize the spiky bluish weed that spelled trouble for mares and their foals. Not only could the weed cause mares to carry foals too long, so that they were too big for a simple birth, but mares who ate fescue could fail to produce milk.

As Sam pictured the entire family patrolling the ten-acre pasture and the new pen with eyes downcast, ready to yank up the weed, Sunny's head snapped up. She rolled her eyes as if she really could sense Sam's feelings.

"It's okay, girl," Sam said, smoothing her hand over the light patches of hair left on Sunny's neck by her freeze brand.

That surge of anxiety and the mare's reaction made Sam think about her decision. Since Dad and Brynna wouldn't help, maybe the vet would.

"Dr. Scott, you know it's time for our cattle drive."

"River Bend, Gold Dust, and Three Ponies," the vet listed the three adjoining ranches. "I heard Maxine Ely will be holding down the fort over at Three Ponies and Ryan, Slocum's boy, will take charge over at Gold Dust." Dr. Scott paused, looking a little skeptical since Ryan Slocum was a teenager newly arrived from England. "Who'll be taking care of things here?"

"Well, it might be me. Do you think I should stay and watch out for Sunny?" Sam asked.

"All alone?"

Sam sighed. There went all the trust she'd thought Dr. Scott had in her.

"I mean," the vet amended, "the mare would probably be fine. Mustangs have been giving birth alone for centuries. I was thinking of you."

The young vet blushed as if he felt awkward considering the welfare of a creature with fewer than four legs.

"Well," Sam admitted, "Mrs. Coley will come over and stay with me, but I'd be in charge of the horses."

"That's fine, then," Dr. Scott said.

Sam made an effort not to roll her eyes. That always annoyed adults. But today was her fourteenth birthday. Anyone should be able to see she didn't need a baby-sitter.

Dr. Scott's hands soothed Sunny as he hunted for the position of the foal. He did this each time he visited, and though he kept talking, his eyes took on a distant, unfocused look.

"I talked to your dad a couple weeks ago. Guess he was thinking about hiring Jake Ely to watch over the ranch, but then he decided he couldn't do it. Said that on a drive, Jake was like his right hand."

Sam felt as if she'd been punched in the stomach. *What about me?*

Luke Ely had six sons at home, all older than she was, to help with his herd. Dad only had Pepper and Ross. She wasn't an experienced cowgirl yet, so of course Dad needed Jake. Still, it hurt. She'd give anything to hear Dad call her his "right hand."

Sam turned away, blinking. If she wanted to be treated like an adult, she couldn't cry like a baby. Dr. Scott didn't seem to notice he'd hurt her feelings.

"Either way," he said, straightening to pat Sunny's shoulder, "I think she'll be fine. But I bet you're planning to stay around."

"I haven't exactly decided," Sam said.

"Have you got that foaling kit together that I told you about? Whoever stays should know where to find it."

"I've got it all together. Do you want to check it?"

"No," the vet said, reaching into his medical bag. "I'm sure you got it right, but I've got another list for you. Give me a call if you notice any of them."

"Okay." Sam took the list and looked it over.

The more she read, the more afraid she got. Could she stay and handle this alone? Her head was spinning.

"Don't go all pale on me now," Dr. Scott said.

If the mare's abdomen suddenly sagged and seemed to develop a sort of point at the lowest part, if she began to look anxiously toward her abdomen, if she pawed the ground and began sweating for no apparent reason . . .

"I'm not," Sam said, but her voice sounded faint, even to her. So much could go wrong.

"Those things are unlikely, but it's her first foal and if the weather gets hot in a hurry, that would increase her odds of an early birth."

"I don't want to rush her," Sam said.

"I'm thinking it will be in three or four days. You've got my cell phone number, so you can get me any time."

He buckled his bag and lifted it, then gave Sam a considering look, as if he knew she couldn't make up her mind.

"My medical opinion is that Dark Sunshine will probably be fine alone. My personal opinion is, I think you'd get a kick out of staying with her. Birthing foals is like nothing else on earth, and you're a natural with horses. You can read them because you care what they're thinking. Dark Sunshine couldn't have a better midwife than you."

Sam was still flying high on the vet's praise at dinnertime. She hadn't completely made up her mind, but she was getting closer.

Seven chairs barely fit around the kitchen table. The swamp cooler that kept them all from heat stroke made a loud, windstormy sound.

Sam watched Jake and Dad poke at her birthday dinner with tentative forks. Gram just laughed at them.

Dad wore a pressed blue shirt with pearl snaps down the front and at the cuffs. Jake's black hair was still damp from a shower and he'd driven over to River Bend Ranch instead of riding. Clearly, they'd both gone to some trouble to look nice for her party, but they were unsure about dinner.

"For heaven's sake, you two," Gram said. "You'd think you'd never eaten a salad before."

"Not instead of dinner," Dad muttered.

"It *is* dinner," Brynna said, rolling her eyes in exaggerated delight. "And it's wonderful!"

Crisp green lettuce was piled high on each plate and topped with ham, cheese, and hard-boiled eggs, for chef's salads.

"I agree!" Jen said. "Even in this heat"—Jen pulled at the neck of her sleeveless turquoise dress to show how hot she was—"my mom's making fried meat and potatoes because that's what Dad likes. This is a civilized meal."

Sam caught Jake's look of disagreement. Maybe he didn't say anything because he'd given Jen a ride to River Bend and had to share the truck cab with her when they left, too. But it was more likely that he didn't want to offend Gram.

Sam watched Jake, noticing how his lips pressed together when he considered the wicker basket of bread sticks. He'd just have to survive on those, his expression said.

"It's a good thing I didn't ask for sushi," Sam joked.

Jake's head snapped up from studying his meal.

"Raw fish?" he asked. "You don't actually eat that, do you?"

Typical, Sam thought. Jake bit his tongue to keep from saying something rude to Gram, but he didn't mind staring at her as if she were nuts.

"It's good," Sam said. "Aunt Sue was just introducing me to it before I left San Francisco." She considered Jake's grimace. "Actually, Jake, I bet you'd like *unagi.*"

"Yeah, I just bet," Jake said. He ate a matchstick-sized piece of cheese before curiosity got the better of him. "Okay, what is it?"

"Eel," Sam said, then laughed along with everyone else when Jake recoiled. "So buckaroos don't eat sushi?"

"Not this one," he said. He shook his head more than the statement required, maybe trying to dispel the image of bite-sized eel.

"Rest assured, we'll have no eel on the trail, Jake," said Gram.

"That's good news," Dad said.

Sam glanced around the kitchen. It looked as it had this time last year when she'd just arrived from San Francisco. Back then, she'd barely noticed the white plastered walls and oak beams because of the cardboard boxes stacked against one wall. Then, she'd wondered what was inside. Now she knew they were packed with the foodstuffs and utensils Gram would need for the cattle drive.

Remembering how Gram had gone ahead of the cattle and riders every day to pitch tents and start the evening meal made Sam long for another week of lowing cows, doe-eyed calves, and endless days in the saddle. She could almost smell the bacon frying over Gram's morning campfires.

"So, are you going on the drive or staying home?" Jen asked suddenly.

The question jerked Sam's mind back into the kitchen. Jen didn't look pushy, but Sam knew her best friend wanted her to go so they could ride together.

"I still haven't exactly made up my mind," Sam admitted.

Jen sighed, but behind her brightly polished glasses, her eyes were filled with understanding.

Jake had just stabbed a piece of ham in his salad. His fork paused halfway to his mouth and he glanced at Dad.

"We're leaving tomorrow at four in the morning," he said.

"So are we," Dad said. "Sam's still figurin' out if that buckskin needs help foaling."

Jake gave a sympathetic nod. At least on horses, Jake and Sam agreed. He knew how excited she was about the coming foal.

"It *is* a tough decision," Brynna said.

She flashed a sympathetic smile that Sam found

really irritating.

"It wouldn't have to be," Sam said. She made sure her voice wasn't defiant, but it didn't keep everyone at the table from looking at her.

"I know," Brynna said. "But I'm excited about going too, Sam, and I can't take any more vacation time yet. I took the week for our honeymoon, and I want to take time when the HARP girls are here."

Brynna gave a small shrug, but it was clear to Sam that there was no way she would change her mind.

"Presents!" Gram said suddenly. "Let's go into the living room to open your gifts, dear, and we can have pie afterward."

The stack of brightly wrapped presents was enough to distract Sam from her dilemma.

Gram loved shopping for clothes and she'd obviously gone back to buy the outfit Sam had spotted at Crane Crossing Mall a few weeks ago. Sam had no idea when she'd wear the short white skirt, matching sandals, and emerald green blouse, but who cared?

"Wow! You remembered! Thanks, Gram!" Sam bounced off the couch and gave Gram a hug before going on to the next present.

Brynna sat on the edge of her chair as Sam dug through the tissue paper–filled gift bag, then pulled out a red leather book with blank pages.

For a moment, Sam didn't know what to say. The book was beautiful, but what was she supposed to do with it?

"You're getting to be such a good photographer, I thought you might like to paste in your favorite pictures, so there's no chance they get lost," Brynna suggested.

"Cool," Jen said with an owlish look. "And you could write captions under them and have a history of your life."

"Thanks," Sam said. She stood and gave Brynna a quick, one-armed hug, too. "It's a great idea."

Her hand hovered over the big white box, battered and clearly recycled from some other gift. It was from Dad. The new chaps he'd given her for the Superbowl of Horsemanship race were supposed to be an early birthday present, so she hadn't expected anything else. She wanted to save this for last.

She picked the decorated envelope from Jen and found it was a gift certificate to her favorite Darton bookstore.

"I feel a shopping trip coming on," Sam said as she hugged Jen.

"Here," Jake said, shoving a box toward her. "This isn't what I wanted to give you, but it was the best thing I could think of."

"With such short notice," Jen murmured sarcastically. "I mean, where did Sam get the idea she could have a birthday *every year*?"

"Jennifer Kenworthy!" Gram's reprimand hid a laugh.

"Sorry, Jake," Jen said, but the way she tossed one blond braid over her shoulder said she wasn't at all contrite. "How were you to know?"

For the thousandth time, she wished her two best friends would quit their sparring. At least they no longer expected her to take sides.

"Wow!" Sam said when she saw the box was filled with rolls of film. "I'll never have to worry about picking which shot I should or shouldn't take."

"That's what my mom said," Jake told her. "She said film comes out of the factory by the mile and a photographer should always take every shot she wants to take."

When Sam stood as if to hug him, too, Jake slammed his spine against the back of his chair. Sam laughed. Jake wasn't into hugs.

At last, she opened Dad's gift, lifting the lid with reverence. For some reason, she knew this present would be special.

It was the tiniest leather halter she'd ever seen. The noseband was so small, Sam didn't think it would encircle her wrist. She knew Dad had made it himself.

"This is the softest leather I've ever felt." Sam ran her fingers over the pale tan straps and looked at the careful stitches Dad had used to fasten them to glittering brass circles.

"Like satin," Brynna said, reaching past Sam to touch it. She looked at Dad with such awe, Sam was sure this gift was a surprise to Brynna as well.

But this meant . . .

Sam didn't ask, but her heart was pounding as hard as if she'd been running. Did this mean what she thought it did?

"It's nothin' to fuss over," Dad said, and his cheeks reddened under his dark tan. "Pretty impractical, but I figured you had your heart set on keepin' that foal—"

Yes, yes, yes!

"—and that bein' the case, you'd better start workin' with it early to keep it from actin' like a jug-headed mustang."

Sam ignored Dad's criticism and tried to think past the sound of her heart's pounding. Dad was giving her the foal.

The Phantom's colt or filly would be hers. Forever.

Suddenly, her decision to stay or go was simple.

Chapter Three ⟋

Sam looked up from the miniature halter. Framed with lines caused by thousands of days of squinting into the Nevada sun, Dad's eyes were dark brown and serious.

"I'm staying," Sam said with determination.

"Thought you might," Dad answered, and though Sam knew he'd feel better having her where he could watch over her, Dad looked satisfied with her decision.

"This calls for a celebration!" Gram said.

Sam laughed aloud. So did Jen and Brynna.

Under his breath, Jake joked, "I'll say."

"Not because you're staying home, dear," Gram amended, giving Sam a kiss on the cheek. "Because I

don't have to ruin your party by telling you to high-
tail it upstairs and start packing!"

"I'll help you with the pie," Brynna said as Gram
started toward the kitchen.

"I'll make coffee," Dad volunteered.

Once they had the living room to themselves,
Sam and Jake and Jen sprawled on the chairs and
couches.

Cougar, Sam's tiger-striped cat, joined them,
sniffing Jen's shoes and rubbing on Jake's jeans
before settling on Sam's lap.

"I sort of envy you," Jen said. "By being the only
one here, you'll get the kind of vet experience I
should be getting. Have you read those books I
loaned you?"

"Cover to cover, more than once," Sam said, glad
she'd accepted Jen's library on horse husbandry. "But
I won't really be alone. Don't forget, Mrs. Coley's
coming over."

"That'll be perfect," Jen said. "She's lived on a
ranch all her life, so she could help if you needed it,
but she's not the sort to get in your way."

Jen was right. If she had to have a baby-sitter,
Mrs. Coley was a good one.

Helen Coley was a friend of Gram's. They
attended the Darton Methodist Church together.
Although Mrs. Coley was housekeeper for Gold
Dust Ranch and chauffeur for Rachel Slocum—who
was a princess in her own mind—Mrs. Coley never

let any of the Slocums dim her smile. .

Mrs. Coley had made Brynna's wedding gown and Sam's bridesmaid dress, but Sam admired her most for another reason. The older woman liked mustangs. In fact, she'd named the Phantom's coal-black son New Moon one day when she'd seen him running with two other young stallions in a bachelor band.

"Could be worse," Sam admitted, then rose to take Jake's empty pie plate. "Let me get you seconds," she said. "You know you want more, and you'll never go ask."

"You are so bossy," Jen said, laughing.

"Am I wrong?" Sam asked Jake.

"No," he said, but he tightened the rawhide string holding his hair back, as if he had to maintain control over something.

Sam heard Dad quietly talking to Brynna, so she paused before going through the swinging door between the living room and kitchen.

"That mare just isn't settling down," Dad said. "That's all that worries me."

"You don't have to—" came Jake's voice from behind Sam when she stopped walking.

She motioned for Jake to stay quiet while she eavesdropped.

"Some mustangs don't," Brynna told Dad. "Her captivity hasn't been a happy one. The first person who adopted her all but ignored her. Then, as soon as she had the title, she sold the mare to that rustler. . . ."

Brynna's voice was hard and angry.

Then, because Brynna remained quiet for a few seconds, Sam leaned closer to the door, closing her eyes to listen more intently. She barely had time to jerk her head out of the way when Brynna opened the door.

"Sam, come in, for heaven's sake. I can hear you breathing."

"It's not Sunny's fault," Sam said.

"Didn't say it was," Dad answered calmly.

Sam felt herself blush. Dad had just given her the best present of her life. There was no way she'd quarrel with him. At least not tonight.

"Sometimes she seems content," Sam said. "Like today, she was rubbing her head against me and she actually wanted me to pet her."

"I really think that this time next year, she'll be fine," Brynna said. "We've got two things working for us. First, the foal. I've heard from adopters that difficult mustang mares develop a sense of home where they foal."

Sam hoped that would work for Dark Sunshine.

"And then there's the HARP program," Brynna said.

"Brynna tells me you'll be working with the buckskin every day, kind of—what did you call it?" Dad asked Brynna. "Showin' the kids?"

"Modeling," Brynna said. "Jake will be telling the girls how to handle the horse—or I will," Brynna added, "and you'll follow directions first, showing them how, before they try."

Sam nodded, looking forward to working with horses every day, but not with Jake in charge. He already thought he had the right to tell her what to do. On the other hand, he might be shy in front of the HARP girls, so it might work out all right.

"She shown any signs of trying to break out?" Dad asked.

"No," Sam said slowly. "But she looks at the mountains a lot. Today we heard a horse neigh and she answered."

She held her breath, but neither Dad nor Brynna looked concerned.

"That's natural," Dad said.

"If she did get loose and went back to the Phantom's herd, what would happen?" Sam asked Brynna.

"Am I assuming you wouldn't put her out there on purpose?" Brynna asked pointedly.

"Oh my gosh, no," Sam said. Even picturing Sunny's sad eyes as she looked toward the Calico Mountains, she knew she wouldn't do it.

What if the Phantom had another lead mare? What if she and Sunny fought?

"Never," Sam said. "She doesn't need any more trauma, you know?"

Brynna and Dad agreed. They knew Sunny had been whipped into obedience, then starved so she'd act as a decoy, leading other mustangs into traps.

Thinking about it, though, Sam knew Sunny's worst suffering hadn't been the physical kind. Time after time, when Sunny finally thought she had a family again, the trapped mustangs were loaded into a truck for illegal sale and she was left behind.

Sam remembered how Sunny's terrible, lonely screams had echoed through Lost Canyon.

"Okay, I'm convinced," Brynna said, touching Sam's arm. "So if she happened to get loose and join up with a free-roaming herd, nothing would happen until we did a gather.

"Then, if she was swept up with other horses, we'd see her freeze brand, check our records, call you up and inform you how much you owed the U.S. government in trespass fees."

"That better not happen," Dad grumbled. "Your allowance for the next three years wouldn't cover it."

Brynna raised her eyes as if making calculations.

"It might," she said.

"I've gotta go talk with Dallas, then I'll check your foaling kit," Dad said. "When you're finished with your friends, come on out. I think Dallas has something for you, too."

"Really?" Sam said. "I thought he was out at Red Rock with Pepper and Ross. Why didn't we ask him in for dinner?"

"We did," Gram said, handing Sam a refilled dessert plate for Jake. "He said he had too much to do before morning, but I believe I heard him mutter something about 'rabbit food,' too."

Chapter Four ⌒

Sam watched her friends drive away. She wouldn't see them for a week, and she'd miss them.

She'd have plenty to do until they returned, though, and after that, they'd be working together with the HARP girls every day.

Right now, she wanted to see what Dad thought of her foaling kit. She started toward the barn, thinking the only good thing about heat and humidity was the way they magnified the smell of sagebrush. She took a deep breath. For her, that scent meant home.

Popcorn and Dark Sunshine stood side by side in the ten-acre pasture. Though the mare only seemed to be tolerating the albino gelding, Sam smiled. Some days were like that, she thought. You just put up with your friends because they were your friends.

At the gate to the pasture, Sam saw Dallas, the ranch foreman. Gray-haired and bow-legged, boots scarred from dust, brush, and stirrups, he couldn't be anything but a cowboy.

He smiled and nodded as she approached. Not only had Dallas known her since she was a baby, he'd helped her find the Phantom when Karla Starr, a dishonest rodeo contractor, had stolen him. Sam knew she could depend on Dallas like a second dad.

Since Dallas had slung Sunny's green halter and a lead rope over the fence, he must be planning to help her move Sunny to her new pasture. That'd be great, but right now Dallas was busy rubbing Amigo behind one ear.

Amigo had been Dallas's favorite mount, but now the sorrel gelding with the graying muzzle was retired. He closed his eyes and leaned into Dallas's touch.

"Happy birthday, cowgirl," Dallas said, then he gave Amigo a last pat and dug into his pocket.

"Thanks," Sam said.

"Now, it's not wrapped, so close your eyes and hold out your hand," he said.

She did. Behind the dark of her eyelids she concentrated on a smell like fresh paint and the lightweight but solid feel of the object Dallas lay gently in her hand.

"Okay, you can look."

Sam did, and saw Dallas had carved a perfect replica of the Phantom.

The palm-sized wooden horse stood proud. His Arab-shaped head lifted to sniff for danger. His high-flung tail drifted on a breeze. Sam had seen the silver stallion just like this, standing on a rim rock, guarding his herd.

"Dallas, he's perfect," Sam said.

"A chunk of wood, whittled with a pocket knife and rubbed with white shoe polish is all it is," he said, shrugging off her compliment.

"It looks just like him," Sam protested.

"Well, it's partly your Blackie," Dallas said, using the name Sam had given the Phantom when he was a foal and she was a child. "And partly another horse."

"His father, Smoke?" Sam guessed.

"No ma'am, his grandsire, I'm pretty sure. Remember your dad talkin' about the Phantom legend, and sayin' there'd always been a fast, couldn't-be-caught white stallion on this range?"

"Sure," Sam said.

"Well, I saw one of those legendary stallions long ago and he woulda left your Blackie in the dust."

Dallas's eyes sparkled in his sun-seamed face and Sam knew he was teasing, but she still had to defend her horse.

"No way," she said.

"Well, your gray is young yet," Dallas admitted. "But I wish you coulda seen the stallion I'm talkin' about.

"I was driving to see my sister who lives way east of here on the other side of the Black Rock Desert. . . ."

Dallas's voice took on a storyteller's cadence as he recalled that day. "I was drivin' along, admirin' the strange desert creatures and the mysterious black mesas that just rear out of the sand and stand alone. I was nearly to Agua Dulce, where my sister lives, when this horse materialized out of the playa. Same color as that white desert floor, almost as if it made him."

Sam shivered. Many times, the Phantom had suddenly appeared, just like that.

"He was a fine-lookin' white stallion, all right, and there was no mistakin' he counted himself the outright *king* of wild horses.

"Of course, I wanted a closer look and since I had brand-new tires on my truck, I steered off the road and followed him across the range. The minute I did, darned if he didn't break into a *pace*. Not a long trot, or a lope, but that gait where both side legs take turns movin' forward and back. Just like those harness-racing horses."

Sam nodded. She'd never seen a pacer, but she could imagine how one would look skimming across the white desert floor, alone.

"When he eased into that pace, he was like a bird flying just above the ground. He wasn't running from me. He was leading me on, I figured out later, hypnotizin' me with that smooth, easy gait.

"I followed him until I got thirsty and reached for the canteen sitting on the seat beside me. I slowed to take that drink, and darned if that stallion didn't stop and wait for me! It was then I realized he was luring me off into the desert."

Amigo had stood quietly listening, but now he whuffled his grassy lips down Sam's forearm and gave her hand a nudge.

"Keep going," she urged Dallas as she petted the old horse.

"Well, I decided not to let that horse have any more fun at my expense," Dallas chuckled. "I drove on to my sister's house and when I told her about the stallion, she gave a yelp. She told me I'd seen the ghost horse. Folks around those parts said he'd punish those who tried to catch him and he did it by losing them in the desert."

"So you were really lucky," Sam said, turning the little carved horse in her hands.

"Not that I believed that story of my sister's," Dallas added. "She's always been sorta gullible."

Sam turned the story over in her mind for a minute. Logic told her a horse wouldn't really do that, but she remembered one night during last year's cattle drive when she'd peered from her sleeping bag to see Slocum and his Thoroughbred Sky returning, beaten, from pursuing the Phantom.

"Still," Dallas went on, looking down at the carved horse, "I tried to give this little critter that same 'don't-you-dare' attitude he had."

"The Phantom does that sometimes," Sam said.

"And that's exactly why," Dallas said, handing

Sam the green halter, "you're gonna be all over his filly and not give her a chance to grow up wild."

Filly? For a minute Sam thought Dallas was talking about Dark Sunshine. Then she realized he meant the foal.

"Filly?" she asked. "You think Sunny's going to have a filly?"

"Oh yeah," Dallas said, as if he had no doubts. "I can tell by the way she's carryin' it."

Sam looked past Amigo across the ten-acre pasture. She had a clear view of Sunny's rounded belly, but it gave her no clues to the foal's gender.

"Have to be a little more experienced, I guess." Dallas gave her a wink, then reached for the wooden horse. "How about I tote this and you go catch her?"

Dark Sunshine watched Sam come. She leaned against the fence, head held low with weariness, and though Popcorn still stood plastered to her side, the mare didn't fuss and nip to drive him away.

"Hey, pretty horses," Sam crooned as she approached.

Popcorn's head bobbed up and his blue eyes watched Sam. The albino was turning into a friendly and interested horse. He wanted to learn and he loved approval.

"Popcorn, I'm sorry I've got to take your friend," she told him as he nudged her shoulder. "But she needs a place of her own to have her baby. Guess what, though?" Sam whispered, and both horses pricked their ears at the sound. "I'll take you for a ride while we're home alone."

Sam glanced back over her shoulder. Only the horses had heard.

She shouldn't have to sneak. After all, both Jen and Brynna had ridden Popcorn and he'd done fine. And neither of them, Sam thought with a smug smile, had ridden a wild stallion whose legs blurred like molten silver.

Sunny let herself be haltered and led from the pasture, in spite of Popcorn's protests and Sweetheart's forlorn neighs.

"They must wonder what's happening to all their friends," Sam said as she led Sunny through the gate Dallas held open.

Sunny stiffened a little at Dallas's nearness, but she didn't shy or refuse to go forward. That was progress.

"These horses'll be callin' back and forth all night long," Dallas grumbled. "I don't know what Wyatt was thinking, moving her tonight when we have to be on the road by four tomorrow morning."

Sam tried to look sympathetic, but couldn't help thinking that even if the bustle of Gram, Dad, and Brynna woke her in the morning, she could roll over and go back to sleep. That would be heavenly.

The foreman shook his head, gave Amigo a good-bye pat, and walked alongside Sam toward the barn pen.

Dad came out to meet them, but he didn't open

the pen gate. He tilted his head, warning Dallas to let Sam do it alone.

Cowboys were just like horses, sometimes, communicating with signs, not sounds.

Alone in her pen, Sunny walked along the fence line until she had a good view of the ten-acre pasture. She whinnied. Three other horses returned her cry.

"Here we go," Dallas muttered.

Sunny walked around her pen, head bobbing from side to side, eyes taking in each post and rock. She launched into a trot, but it only lasted a few hammering steps. Then her eyes and lips tightened in an expression Sam recognized as a wince.

"She's too far along for that to feel good," Dad said. "Carrying an extra hundred pounds mostly in one spot is gonna slow her down."

It didn't keep Sunny quiet, though. As Sam sorted through the foaling kit, reciting the use of each item for Dad's approval, she raised her voice over the noisy horses.

"Here's Dr. Scott's phone number, and a pad and paper to write down observations, so that I can answer his questions."

Dad nodded.

"I've got sterile cotton, Ivory soap, and I put a bucket with a lid in by the stall. Here are my plastic gloves . . ."

Sam described the supplies, ending with a white terry cloth towel.

". . . and a fresh towel with no scent, so that when I dry off the foal, she'll still smell like a horse, not fabric softener."

"She?" Dad asked, smiling. "So you've decided it's a filly, have you?"

"Dallas did," Sam told him.

"Well then, you'd better start thinking up filly names," Dad said. "He's usually right."

Dallas touched the brim of his hat in acknowledgment, then held up a lantern he'd retrieved from Blackbeard's Closet.

"Thanks," Sam said, and Dallas smiled at her enthusiasm.

Even though she'd had to clean Blackbeard's Closet for punishment pretty recently, the cabinet was still so crammed full, opening the door guaranteed an avalanche of miscellaneous stuff.

"Likely as not this storm will blow past us and you won't lose power," Dallas said. "But in the old days, before we had that fancy overhead lighting, this is how we watched a mare in labor. I'm puttin' this in the tack room, just in case."

Dallas shrugged off her thanks and dug into his pocket for the white wooden horse. He regarded it for a minute.

"Tell ya what I'm going to do," he said, then stood tall and reached his arm over his head. "I'll put him up here."

Sam frowned in confusion as Dallas balanced the

carving on a board above the barn door, but then he explained.

"If a horseshoe's good luck, a whole horse outta be ten times better."

"Thanks," Sam said again, but Dallas was already walking off on some errand of his own.

"Old cowboys can be sorta superstitious," Dad said, shaking his head.

Sam made a small sound of agreement, as Dad went on.

"We need to talk about a couple other things, in case things don't go as planned," Dad said, leading the way to the tack room.

Sam realized she was holding her breath. She liked being trusted, but she wasn't sure about taking on *this* much responsibility. Dark Sunshine had already had a tough life. She shouldn't have to depend on a beginner to help her through this.

"Now don't worry," Dad said. He must have read her worried expression. "Horses have foaled for a million years or so without help. Sometimes folks just mess things up instead of helping, but since this is Sunny's first foal, you need to be prepared. Giving birth can be scary for young mares."

Dad pointed to the green halter she'd taken from Sunny's head.

"Keep her halter at hand. That way, if she won't let the foal nurse, you can try to hold her still. If she fights you, ask Helen Coley to help you put on a twitch. She'll know how."

Sam stiffened at the suggestion.

The twitch was a short, smooth stick with a soft loop of cord at one end. When a horse refused to stand still for the blacksmith or vet, its top lip could be inserted through the loop. Then the stick was twisted.

That was only supposed to distract the horse. Sam touched her own lip and twisted. It didn't hurt much, but she sure didn't like it.

"If she still won't stand without kicking at the baby, you need Dr. Scott." Dad's eyes locked on hers. "It's vital that the foal drink the mare's milk. It will give her the nutrition she needs to survive."

"Got it," Sam said, but she was imagining the cozy pictures of mares and foals she'd seen in Jen's books, and hoping Sunny would simply cooperate.

Blaze yapped from the ranch yard. Then, mouth open and tail wagging in a wide circle, he frisked into the barn just ahead of Brynna.

Her stepmother still wore her work clothes. Her red braid was unraveling over the shoulder of her khaki uniform, but her smile showed above the stack of folded blankets she carried.

"I'm so glad I remembered these before I got into bed. I have a habit of doing that," she confided. "Once I pull up the covers and close my eyes, my mind kicks into high gear."

"Good timing," Dad said. "I was just about to show her the cot."

Dad lifted a brand-new folding bed from a box in the tack room.

"Since most mares foal a couple hours before dawn, I figured you'd be wanting to sleep out here," Dad said.

"Helen Coley knows you have our permission," Brynna put in.

"Might as well be comfortable," Dad added.

Sam couldn't believe it. The halter, the vet bills, and now this. Dad was spending a lot of money on Sunny's foal.

Sam couldn't find the words to tell Dad how much this meant to her, so she tackled him with a hard hug.

He gave her back a flat-handed pat and didn't seem to mind talking to the top of her head.

"You be careful of that mare. Don't take anything for granted. If she gets a chance to skedaddle, I think she will. I'm not sure you'll ever get the wildness out of her. She just doesn't see the profit in it."

Sam looked up. "I'm not sure what you mean."

"Take Ace, for example," Dad said. "He likes his regular meals and he likes you. But the mare's early days with people were nothing to brag about, and she still seems to expect the worst."

While Dad and Brynna helped Gram load the last of the supplies into the white van, which had been converted into a modern-day chuck wagon, Sam stood at the fence of the barn corral.

It was far too hot for an early summer evening. The fence boards still held warmth from the day's high temperatures and night felt more like a dark blanket than cool shade. No wind stirred the leaves on the cottonwood trees or blew Dark Sunshine's mane as she ripped at the grass, shaking her head when a bite had dirt clinging to it.

A mosquito whined past Sam's cheek. As she brushed it away, a movement caught her eye and she saw cookie-cutter-perfect wings against a bruise-colored sky. A bat.

"Help yourself to as many mosquitoes as you want," Sam said, thinking about the nights she'd spend in the barn. "And bring your friends."

Her voice didn't echo. It sounded dull, as if the low-hanging clouds could deaden sound.

Maybe this was the calm before the storm, Sam thought, but it didn't feel calm.

It felt as if the sky was holding its breath, waiting until she was all alone to cut loose.

Chapter Five ⌒∾

"Sam, get up." Brynna's voice cut through Sam's dream.

Sam lifted her wrist. She knew her watch's glowing numbers were right in front of her face, but it took a few seconds before she managed to open her eyes.

It was three-thirty on a summer morning. Actually, she was pretty sure three-thirty still counted as night.

"What?" Sam asked.

Then, before Brynna could answer, Sam's legs pedaled beneath the covers, trying to get going. What if Dark Sunshine was foaling?

"I want to see you ride Popcorn."

"What?" Sam asked again, but this time she was sitting up, rubbing her eyes.

"Since Ace is already out at Red Rock, and you'll want to ride this week, I thought you'd want to try Popcorn instead of one of the older horses."

"Yeah." Sam rested her feet on the floor and stood. She looked down at what she'd worn to bed, wondering if Popcorn would object to her T-shirt and boxer-style shorts.

"We're driving out of the yard in twenty-two minutes." Brynna's voice sharpened and Sam knew it was meant to spur her along. "Show me you can catch, saddle, and ride him now, and you have permission to ride him while we're gone. If not, I'm telling Helen Coley you can only ride Sweetheart."

Brynna's feet were tapping down the staircase by the time Sam opened a dresser drawer.

Oh right, like Brynna's going to call Helen Coley now, Sam thought. But she'd been aching to ride Popcorn, so she'd do it. Still, couldn't Brynna have had this brainstorm yesterday afternoon?

Sam pulled on some jeans and made her way downstairs to find Gram and Dad standing in the kitchen with cups of coffee, watching Blaze. The Border collie's muzzle lay on his crossed paws and no matter what they said or did, his plumy tail barely moved.

"He knows you're leaving without him," Sam said through a yawn.

Gram nodded and Dad looked pointedly at the kitchen clock.

"I'm hurrying," Sam insisted.

In spite of the front porch light, she couldn't see horses in the ten-acre pasture. It was that dark.

Gradually, Popcorn's pale body took shape and so did the light patches on Sweetheart's pinto coat.

And there was Brynna. She'd decided to speed things up by gathering tack and a can of grain. All of the horses stood at the gate, ears pricked forward with interest.

"Thanks," Sam said as she took the halter and grain.

In minutes, she had the big albino tied at the hitching rail. Except for three pulls toward Dark Sunshine's corral, he stood quietly.

He didn't want to accept the snaffle, but Sam nudged the toothless bar of his jaw with her finger and he opened his mouth to accept the bit. While she lifted the bridle up, gently bent his white ears beneath the headstall, and adjusted the throat latch, he watched her with trusting blue eyes.

"You're a good boy," Sam told him.

Once she'd saddled Popcorn, she mounted slowly, giving the mustang time to feel her weight in the stirrup before she swung aboard and settled on his back.

"He's perfect," Sam said as she guided the gelding in a wide circle around Brynna. "See?"

"Ride him out to the bridge and back," Brynna instructed. "I'm going to surprise him, so be ready."

"Got it," Sam said. She swallowed hard, but she didn't ask what kind of surprise.

Popcorn's head jerked up. His ears flicked forward, back, and sideways, showing he wasn't quite sure about all this. Still, he obeyed.

Sam knew why Brynna wanted to surprise the gelding while he was carrying her.

"It's to test me, not you," she told the horse.

Popcorn still responded better to plow reining than neck reining, so she pulled her right hand out, away from her body, and he followed it, turning back toward the ranch house.

Instantly Sam noticed Brynna seemed to have vanished.

Where was she? Was Brynna going to hide and pop out waving her hands and yelling?

No. Brynna's single step was enough to scare the albino.

She'd been standing right next to one of the porch posts. As she moved away from it, Popcorn saw a thing that had seemed solid, suddenly divide.

He shied, but Sam used her legs to drive him forward.

"C'mon boy, no big deal."

Popcorn tried to sidestep, but she tightened her legs even more and he went on. Sam only let him slow when he came even with Brynna. He swung his head to study her, then sneezed and swished his tail, seeming almost embarrassed.

"Great," Brynna said. She looked away as the kitchen door opened and Dad and Gram emerged. "I think she's good to go."

"Never doubted it," Dad said, but the way Brynna regarded him, hands on hips, said otherwise.

"Come on down so I can hug you good-bye, honey," Gram said.

Popcorn hung at the end of the reins, wary as he watched the flurry of arms and kisses.

Red taillights were bobbing across the bridge, growing smaller, disappearing, by the time Sam realized she was one day past fourteen years old and in charge of an entire ranch.

She turned Popcorn back into his pasture to be nosed by Sweetheart and Amigo. Then she fed the horses and checked their water. She hadn't heard a peep from the chickens, so she didn't disturb them.

When the glossy-feathered Rhode Island Red rooster came out crowing, it would be time to gather eggs.

"Until then," Sam said to Blaze, who leaned against her legs as if trying to trip her, "why don't we go inside for a little breakfast?"

Sam meant to make something sweet and unwholesome for breakfast, but once Blaze was consoling himself with a dog cookie, she thought of an even more forbidden treat. A nap.

She'd lie down on the couch for a few minutes, before it started getting hot outside. As soon as she stretched out, Cougar appeared. With a mew, he asked permission, then vaulted onto her stomach. With precise steps, he walked up to collapse on her chest.

To the sound of Cougar's purring, Sam fell back to sleep.

Someone was knocking on the kitchen door.

Blaze was barking.

Hazy light at the living room windows gave Sam no clue to time. It could have been six in the morning or six at night.

It was nearly eight, Sam saw when she glanced at the clock as she rushed through the kitchen toward the door. She could see Mrs. Coley's shiny gray hair through the door window.

"Hi," Sam said, sounding groggy.

A gust of hot wind came in along with Mrs. Coley.

"Don't wear that guilty expression for me," Mrs. Coley said.

Sam rubbed a hand over her sleep-mashed hair and straightened her T-shirt.

"I could see the horses had been fed. And the hens looked happy chasing grasshoppers out of Grace's garden. That's good enough for me."

"Sunny—" Sam began.

"The little buckskin?" Mrs. Coley set a covered

plate on the table and turned toward the refrigerator. "She hasn't foaled yet, if that's what you're wondering.

"Grace told me she was due," Mrs. Coley explained. "But to tell you the truth, Samantha, I've never known a mare to foal during daylight hours. Actually, it's a good thing you had a little nap so you'll be more alert tonight. Now, before you go out and get busy, why don't we have some cookies and milk?"

Mrs. Coley had made big soft oatmeal cookies full of nuts and dried cranberries. They made a perfect breakfast.

"We're supposed to have dry lightning this afternoon and an absolute frog strangler of a storm tomorrow," Mrs. Coley said.

"Storms don't scare me," Sam said. "It will be a relief."

Suddenly she was glad Brynna had insisted Mrs. Coley spend the nights with her. Sleeping in the barn with Sunny during a summer shower would be fun with Mrs. Coley in the house, for backup, ready to help or call Dr. Scott.

"It will be a relief," Mrs. Coley agreed. "But that new barn"—Mrs. Coley gestured toward Gold Dust Ranch—"has gaps in the roof. My employer hired a Cincinnati builder who specialized in 'architecturally unique structures,' but he'd never built a barn before," Mrs. Coley explained. "It's a pretty building, but it has some flaws in terms of housing livestock."

Sam wasn't surprised. Linc Slocum was rarely

willing to take advice from more experienced cattle-men, even though he'd kept Jed Kenworthy, Jen's dad, on as foreman after he bought his ranch.

"That Ryan is as broody as a mother hen about Hotspot," Mrs. Coley said, smiling. "He's been calling Dr. Scott every day, because he's afraid Hotspot can't foal safely if the roof leaks."

Until a few months ago, Linc Slocum's son Ryan had lived in England with his mother. Unlike Linc, Ryan was a horseman and he'd fallen in love with Apache Hotspot. The blue-blooded Appaloosa mare had arrived in an air-conditioned horse van at the end of last summer, but right away she'd been stolen by a hammerhead stallion.

Linc had promised to give Sam the foal, but if Ryan wanted it, there was no doubt in Sam's mind that it would belong to him.

I already have enough horses, Sam told herself, though she didn't really believe it.

Ace was hers. Sunny's foal would be, too. And even though Sunny's role was to help girls in the HARP program, the mare had come closest to bond-ing with her.

". . . taken it into his head to patch that roof him-self since his father didn't hire it done before he left for the cattle drive," Mrs. Coley was saying.

"What?" Sam asked. Her mind had wandered, wondering if she'd ever have *enough* horses.

"That's why I have to go back over to Gold Dust

for a little while," Mrs. Coley said. "That boy's going up on the barn roof with shingles, and it's just not safe to do that alone."

"Isn't Rachel home?" Sam asked.

"Well, yes," Mrs. Coley began.

Ryan's twin, Rachel, was her daddy's princess. Model-sleek and pretty, Rachel pampered herself with the finest clothes and makeup and she despised horses and ranch life.

Sam would hate to have to depend on Rachel in an emergency.

"Forget I asked," Sam said.

If Ryan fell from the roof, an ambulance would have to come all the way from Darton. It would be smart to call the volunteer fire department, too, because its members were trained first responders and lived within minutes of the ranch.

In an emergency, Mrs. Coley would know what to do. Rachel wouldn't have a clue.

"So I'll just run back over there," Mrs. Coley said, standing. "But I'll be back here before dark. And don't worry about dinner. I'll bring something with me."

"I'll be fine," Sam said, following Mrs. Coley outside.

It would be great to have the ranch to herself. After her chores were finished, she might take Sunny down to wade in the river.

Mrs. Coley studied the sky, then looked west,

beyond the ridge that ran behind the Gold Dust, River Bend, and Three Ponies ranches. A metallic flicker showed faraway lightning.

Lightning could cause fires. Sunny had already had to run for her life once because of a fire.

What if the lightning signaled an approaching hailstorm? Sam had seen the damage their icy pounding could cause.

And Mrs. Coley had said the storm was supposed to be a "frog strangler." A heavy downpour could cause the La Charla River to flood. The last time it had, a wall of water had rushed over the ranch, killing cattle, changing the landscape with huge rolling boulders, and nearly drowning Sam and Ace.

There'd been a power failure and the roads had been washed out, too.

If that happened this time, she'd be marooned on the ranch alone.

With a flurry of feathers, the red hens rushed away from Gram's garden. The hot wind plucked at their wings and they packed into their henhouse with worried clucks.

"It's a good thing you're not afraid of storms," Mrs. Coley said, giving Sam a thumbs-up sign, "'cause I think this one is going to be a doozie."

"Yep," Sam said as Mrs. Coley got into the car and thunder rumbled overhead. "Good thing."

Chapter Six ⟩

$\mathcal{D}$ad and the cowboys hadn't left her very many chores, so Sam did as Gram had asked, watering the garden and plucking out the hopeful green weeds that had sprouted overnight.

While she weeded, Blaze found a patch of shade nearby and dug into the dirt with his nose. He lay down, leaving his muzzle there, eyes watching Sam.

She wanted to lead Sunny down to the La Charla. It was a short walk, just enough exercise for the weary mare, and the cool water would soothe the delicate legs that were supporting an extra burden.

As Sam worked her fingers into the earth around Gram's tomato plants, she watched the ridge. The lightning that glimmered in the west hadn't come again. At least not when she'd been watching.

Her brow was sweaty from the rare humidity of an approaching storm, and the cool river appealed to her, too. But was it safe? She wished she had someone to ask, but she didn't.

This was the downside of being in charge. If she stood beside Sunny through the safe delivery of a healthy foal, she'd get all the credit. But if something went wrong, she'd get the blame.

"What do you think, Blaze?" Sam asked the Border collie.

His white-tipped tail thumped and he raised his muzzle. Small clumps of dirt fell from it as he panted hopefully.

"Me too," she said. "Let's go."

She entered Sunny's pen from the barn. Last night she'd only led the mare in and out through the fence. It was important that Sunny knew she could be released into the pen from her stall. Sam wanted Sunny to stay calm during the birth and after her foal was born. Appearing from a strange entrance could startle her.

"Hey, girl," Sam said, coming from the dark barn into the sunlit pen. "Want to play in the river?"

Sam stood still when the buckskin noticed her. Sunny took a dozen deliberate steps her way, but stopped just out of petting range.

"You feel safer when there's a fence between us, girl?"

The mare looked beyond her with such intensity, Sam glanced back over her shoulder.

There was nothing there but the hillside leading up to the ridge, covered with sagebrush and sun-bleached grass. There was no movement except for a few clumps of white prickly poppies that quaked in the faint, hot wind.

When she looked back, Sunny was studying her. Sam looked into the mare's eyes, glad to see that the wild loneliness was gone. She remembered when Sunny had looked vicious. Now she was only cautious.

"Jen's books say you can have mood swings just before you have your baby," Sam said as she eased the green halter on the mare. "But I'm not seeing any."

The mare jerked away. The lead rope snaked a few inches through Sam's hands before she gripped, but Sunny was only grabbing a mouthful of grass.

"I'll make you a bran mash when we get back, okay? Gram left me the recipe."

She led the mare back through the barn, stopping in the big box stall. Last night, since there'd been no signs Sunny was on the verge of giving birth, Dad had advised Sam to leave the mare outside so she could still see the other horses while she got used to the new enclosure.

"Tonight, you're sleeping in here," Sam told her.

The mare watched dust dance in the shafts of faint dusty sunlight sifting through the roof.

Their barn roof wasn't solid, either, but Sam knew the mare wouldn't be drenched in a downpour. Since the earthquake, the entire barn had been repaired by professionals.

Overhead, a pigeon cooed. Sunny looked up. Her forelock fell away from her tawny face and she blinked.

"You don't look like a crazy girl anymore," Sam told the mare.

Sunny sniffed as if the very idea was ridiculous, and Sam laughed.

"This foaling's going to be as simple as can be, right?"

This time the mare just leaned against the lead rope. When Sam gave a step, Sunny headed for the barn door, towing Sam after her.

Cool air wafted from the river. For a few minutes, Sunny was content to wade, but then she started acting funny.

"What do you want, girl?"

The mare shook. She dropped the shoulder nearest the water, then shook her mane. She struck at the mud and stepped back as her hoof hit a rounded river rock.

Suddenly Sam realized the mare wanted to roll in the mud. It was too rocky here, but she saw a bare stretch of shoreline.

"I don't know, girl," she said, looking at the mare's unwieldy body.

But what could it hurt? Dr. Scott had said mares often got up and down many times while they were giving birth. She might as well practice.

It turned out she'd read Sunny's intentions exactly right. As soon as her hooves touched the cool, bare sand, the mare lowered herself with a groan.

Sam held the very end of the lead rope, to stay out of range of the mare's hooves as she rolled, splashing in the shallows.

With a huge sigh, Sunny lay on her side. Her eyes closed.

Sam stayed quiet. She rarely saw horses rest on their sides this way. She'd always assumed it had to do with survival. If you slept standing on your four legs, you'd be set to escape a predator. If you slept on your side, you had to get those long, gangly legs arranged, rock to your feet, and *then* try to outrun danger.

To rest like this, Sunny must be exhausted. Sam looked at the sleek, golden-brown shoulder and wanted to stroke it. She wanted to remind Sunny that the human hand could do more than hurt. Instead, she let her sleep.

While the mare dozed, Sam gazed across the rippling La Charla River. The cattle had been gathered and she saw no mustangs, but something told her the Phantom wasn't far away.

With luck, one of his older, experienced mares had become lead mare. According to Dallas, even Queen, the red dun, had been young for the job. And she was about five when the Bureau of Land Management had taken her, injured, from the range.

Sam tried to recall the Phantom's mares. She

closed her eyes, picturing a pair of blood bays, a sorrel, a buckskin, several dark bays, and a big honey-colored mare she'd seen up close. Too close.

On Dad and Brynna's wedding day, Sam had taken a spill on the range, and though much of the herd had split around her, the big mare had jumped right over her.

Far-off thunder rumbled and Sunny's ears twitched in her sleep. On the range, that sound would probably have been a sign to seek shelter. With another heavy sigh, the mare lurched to her feet and stared around as if she didn't remember coming here.

Mood swings didn't have to mean cranky and snappish, Sam guessed. Maybe Sunny's calm confusion counted, too.

"Let's go get the mud brushed out of your coat," Sam said.

Back in the barn, the mare welcomed grooming as if it were a massage. Every few minutes, she grabbed a bite of the wheat straw, but she seemed tranquil.

Suddenly, though, her head rose and her eyes widened. Nostrils flaring, she moved toward the opening into the pen. She took determined steps, fully awake now, and Sam followed.

Sunny's attention focused on the ridge.

Sam thought of cougars, coyotes, and wild horse rustlers.

"You're safe, girl," she told Sunny, but she wasn't so sure.

Sam glanced over her shoulder to see Blaze was dozing on the front porch. If Sunny sensed something threatening, Blaze would be jetting through the ranch yard after it.

Sunny gave two huffs through her nostrils, then nickered.

"I don't see—"

And then she did.

A tall copse of mountain mahogany made a spiky interruption to the ridgeline. Beyond it, she saw a flicker of white. What she saw wasn't prickly poppies growing on the hillside beyond this one, nor a wisp of cloud in the sullen sky. High on the ridge, where she'd never seen him before, stood the Phantom.

He was at least a mile away, but she saw the glint of silver as he arched his neck, and the glittering strength of his shoulder muscles in the strange summer light. He seemed to prance in place, showing off, but he moved no closer.

What is he doing here?

Not since the accident that had set him free had the stallion returned to River Bend Ranch.

Dallas had told her that some nights when she was in San Francisco and he'd been up late, sitting on the bunkhouse step, playing his guitar, he'd seen an iron-gray horse at the river. He'd thought it might be her colt. After a while, the horse had quit coming. He might have joined a mountain herd, Dallas had said. Or maybe, Dallas had joked, the horses disapproved of the switch in music. Dallas had taken to playing the harmonica, because his arthritis made fretting the guitar difficult.

She'd seen the stallion many places, but never here. Still, his willingness to move around had probably contributed to his healthy herd.

Brynna said that a lot of wild horses stayed in one place, even when water and graze dwindled.

The Phantom moved from his hidden valley to a plain above War Drum Flats, and a streamside green strip in Arroyo Azul. But he shouldn't be here.

Sunny's ears flattened. Sam wondered whether she should touch the mare to comfort her. Just then Sunny's hind legs kicked in a signal that she didn't want company, even the Phantom's.

"Good girl," Sam said. "It's the wrong time to run off and play. You tell him."

Sam couldn't believe what she'd just said. She felt a frown tighten between her eyes.

What if the Phantom had come for *her*? What if he knew the other humans were gone, that she was alone and he needn't fear capture?

She couldn't let him venture onto the ranch that had once been his home. His presence would agitate Dark Sunshine. The mare didn't look eager to join him, but what if she changed her mind? Sam imagined herself trying to restrain Sunny as she tried to escape. And if she did break out, Sunny couldn't run with him. She'd strain, then fall behind. Nothing about his visit would be good for the foal.

And there was danger in letting the Phantom come to a civilized place. He'd been captured before when he'd grown too trusting.

Don't come down here, Sam told him silently.

He stood so statue still, Sam's eyes darted to the clouds above the ridge. White thunderheads sculpted with silver were mounded behind him. When the Phantom's mane lifted on the breeze, it blended with the clouds.

Hypnotized by the mustang merging with his surroundings, it took Sam a minute to realize what she heard.

A quiet crack, then another. Plopping sounds, then patters. Rain began to fall on dry grass, fence posts, Sunny, and Sam.

The stallion turned. His tail drifted like a swan's wing, and then he was gone.

Sam stayed beside Dark Sunshine. She didn't speak, didn't pull on the lead rope or coax the mare to do anything. Sunny had discouraged the stallion. She'd done what was best for her foal.

Sam watched, knowing the mare would show her the next step.

Suddenly the mare flinched and glanced back toward her belly. The foal had probably kicked inside her, Sam decided, when Sunny swished her black tail and fell to grazing.

"Time for that bran mash?" Sam asked quietly.

In response, Sunny lifted her head. The single-minded concentration with which she'd been eating during the last two weeks seemed to have faded. Now, she followed Sam back into the barn.

Sam closed the gate to the small pasture and locked it. She turned on the overhead lights so Sunny would be used to them by the time they were necessary. Then Sam left for the house.

She'd measured out the bran, grated carrots, and oil and begun steaming the mash when there was a crackle of lightning. The kitchen lights flickered. Sam stopped, waiting to see if they'd lose power. When they didn't, she proceeded with the recipe just as Gram had shown her.

She was concentrating so hard, she jumped when the phone rang.

"Sam, I'm sorry I'm so late."

It was Mrs. Coley.

Sam glanced at the kitchen clock, surprised to see it was four o'clock. Weeding and spending time with Dark Sunshine had soaked up most of the day. The way the sun had hidden behind the clouds all day had fooled her.

"That's okay," Sam said. It probably wouldn't be polite to say she hadn't noticed, so she added, "I've been busy."

"You haven't seen that white stallion, have you?"

Sam caught her breath. Dozens of thoughts ricocheted through her mind, but they all felt the same. *Something's wrong.*

"Why?" Sam asked.

"We saw him on the ridge up behind the house," Mrs. Coley said. "And since it runs behind your place, too, I thought I'd check. You don't want to lose that buckskin mare at this stage."

Sam agreed, but then she heard an adamant male voice saying something in the background.

"Ryan would like to talk with you, Sam," Mrs. Coley said, and something about her tone held a warning.

"Okay—"

"Samantha, we have a problem." Ryan's voice was clipped and tense and very clearly implied the problem was hers to fix.

Chapter Seven ❧

We have a problem.

Sam exhaled. For some reason, her mind didn't search for the way Dad or Gram would handle this. She thought of Jake.

When things went wrong, Jake didn't show it. He looked relaxed, almost sleepy. That made people around him calm down.

I can do that, Sam thought. She closed her eyes and made her voice lazy.

"What problem is that?" she asked.

"That 'Phantom stallion'"—Ryan's tone was condescending, as if he were talking about a cartoon hero—"is up to his old tricks."

Take a deep breath, Sam told herself. She pictured

Jake with his eyelids half lowered.

"Yeah?" she asked.

"Indeed. He's trying to steal domestic mares again."

"Wait just a minute!" Sam snapped. "What are you talking about?"

"You know very well what I'm talking about," Ryan began.

"You weren't here when that hammerhead stallion came sneaking around trying to assemble a harem," she accused. As an angry flush heated her skin, she knew the Jake technique would never work for her.

"Blaming another stallion is a fairy tale—"

"I saw him with my own eyes. I photographed him—"

"Yes, yes, I've heard all about it, but I have a valuable mare—" Ryan's voice broke off.

Had he heard how much he sounded like his father? Did he realize he'd tried to disguise his feelings with talk of money?

In the minute they were both quiet, Sam heard the patter of rain turn to a steady downpour. A rumble of far-off thunder sounded like a lion's growl.

"I just thought," Ryan said, finally, "it would be wise to notify you of the stallion's presence, since you, too, have a mare in delicate condition."

Ryan hadn't exactly backed down, but he hadn't tried very hard to change her mind, either.

"Thank you," Sam said. "I'll keep my eyes open."

Her lips had parted to say good-bye when Mrs. Coley came back on the line.

"You can see why I've been delayed getting back to your place. He's very nervous," she said quietly.

"I guess I understand," Sam said.

"Hotspot's overdue and she'll foal tonight. I'm sure of it. I'm *not* sure he's up to dealing with her alone."

Panic mixed with Sam's pride that Mrs. Coley thought she *was* up to dealing with a foaling mare. She'd counted on having an experienced adult as backup.

Not even an adult. Jake would have been fine, or Jen. . . .

"I know you're new to this, too," Mrs. Coley said. "But your buckskin comes from a long line of hardy mares. They gave birth on the range, in spite of snow, sandstorms, and hungry predators, then returned to the herd and moved on.

"Hotspot's parents were probably raised in stables more luxurious than our houses. Besides, horses are in your blood, Sam."

"Thanks," Sam said, though she found herself peeking at the gummy bran mash so she wouldn't feel embarrassed by the praise.

Blaze lifted his head and sniffed, deciding whether her concoction was something he wanted to sample.

"Now, you call me for anything at all," Mrs. Coley said firmly. "Unless we run into trouble with this mare, I'll be over there before you go to bed."

Low-hanging clouds and rain made the afternoon feel like evening. Sam left the kitchen lights on, since it might be full dark by the time she returned from the barn.

Hands covered in oven mitts, Sam jogged from the house to the barn, carrying the mash. She was soaked. Her hair was plastered to her head, but the bran mash was still hot by the time she got across the ranch yard.

As soon as she saw Dark Sunshine, she forgot all about the bran mash except to set it down and start shucking off the mitts.

The barn was dim, but she could see the little buckskin staring painfully at her side.

Sam flicked on the overhead lights. The switch didn't move. It was already on. So why were the lights out?

She moved back to the barn door and squinted through the rain at the house.

She was positive she'd left the kitchen lights on, but the house was dark.

Sunny pawed furiously with one hoof. She kept watching her side, then walked a tight circle around the box stall.

It was then that Sam noticed the damp bedding in

one corner of the stall. The bag of waters the foal had lived in for eleven months had been ruptured by the foal's eager movements. It was ready to be born.

Elation and alarm rushed through Sam. Very soon, she would see the Phantom's foal!

"Here we go, girl," she told Sunny, then Sam sat down to wait.

When Sunny lowered herself to lie in the wheat straw, Sam realized how much she was squinting. Dallas—and all the books—had said it was important to watch the mare closely. Foals could enter the world in all sorts of contorted positions, which usually required a vet's help. The sooner you noticed, the safer the baby would be.

Sam jumped up and retrieved the lantern Dallas had left in the tack room. She pumped the handle, lit the wick, then adjusted a silver knob until a bright, steady flame illuminated the stall.

Blaze had followed her to the barn. He sniffed disapprovingly at the scent of lantern fuel, but Sunny didn't notice.

Still resting on her side, the mare closed her eyes. Her legs folded, then extended. With each thunderclap and sizzle of lightning, she jerked awake.

"It's not that close," Sam whispered to the mare.

Then, to comfort herself, she used the little formula Gram had taught her.

With the next flash of lightning, she counted

slowly. "One thousand, two thousand, three thousand, four thousand, five—"

Boom!

According to Gram, each time you got to five thousand, the lightning was one mile away. As Sam considered what that meant, she swallowed hard. And another boom sounded.

To cover the furious sounds outside, Sam sang. She tried cowboy songs, but every one she could remember was depressing. "Bury Me Not on the Lone Prairie" wasn't what a mustang wanted to hear. Neither was "The Streets of Laredo," though a cowboy, not a horse, lay dying in that song.

Weren't there any cheerful cowboy songs? Wait, maybe she had one.

"Oh my darlin', oh my darlin', oh my darlin' Clementine, you are lost and gone forever . . ."

No. Definitely not.

"Sorry, girl," Sam apologized as Sunny launched herself back to her feet.

Sam wanted to call Mrs. Coley, but why should she? Sunny was behaving exactly as Dad, Dr. Scott, and the books said she should.

More restless than pained, Sunny kept moving around, trying to stay comfortable as the foal positioned itself for birth.

All at once, Blaze bounced to his feet. In the same instant, Sam felt the hair on her arms lift as if she'd taken off a staticky sweater. Then, the air turned blue, the barn shuddered, and—*boom*!

Sam's ears ached as if she'd been thrust to the bottom of a swimming pool.

Sunny's eyes rolled white. She braced her legs and neighed. Outside, Amigo, Popcorn, and Sweetheart answered with frightened calls.

Sam swallowed the scream in her own throat.

Get a grip, she told herself. It was a lightning strike and a thunderclap. Close. That's all.

Once the sounds had rolled into silence, Sunny's fear appeared to vanish. Her attention turned inward again. She had her foal to think about.

But what had caused that blue flash? Lightning hitting the house? The bunkhouse? A cottonwood tree that would flare into flame and set everything else on fire?

Sam peered cautiously from the barn doorway and Blaze leaned against her legs. Sparks gnawed along the power lines, bright as Fourth of July fireworks. But not for long. As she watched, the electrical fire sputtered, then disappeared, extinguished by the rain.

"It's okay," she told Blaze. "The power's already out and now the fire is, too."

Sam had only taken a couple of steps away from the barn door when another thought popped into her mind. What if that wasn't a power pole?

She stared at it again. How could she tell the difference between a power pole and a telephone pole?

It didn't matter, she told herself. She either had

telephone service or she didn't. Running to the house to check would make no difference.

None.

But she had to know.

Sunny was flicking her tail and stamping her hind hooves as if she wanted to kick.

"I'll be right back, Sunny," Sam promised. "I won't stop for anything. I'll pick up the telephone, listen, and hang up. I promise."

The mare didn't care. Her eyes were wide but her attention was turned inward.

Sam ran. She splashed through the puddles. She felt exposed, as if a lightning bolt were aimed right between her shoulder blades.

I'm halfway safe, she thought as she clattered up the front porch steps and into the kitchen. Crossing every finger, she closed her eyes and lifted the receiver.

Nothing.

She replaced the receiver and lifted it again. Still no dial tone. It *had* been a telephone pole. There was no way to summon help.

Run. Responsibility crashed down on her, and each drop of rain told her to hurry. Dark Sunshine had no one to count on now except for her.

Sam burst back into the barn and pushed her dripping hair away from her face to see Sunny lying on her side, legs straight and stiff. Contractions rippled over her belly.

"I'm here, girl," she whispered to the mare. "That may not sound like much, but I know everything books and cowboys can teach me, and I love you."

As if in response, Sunny half stood. Her front legs trembled with effort and she gave Sam a beseeching stare.

Then, with a slither and a thud, enclosed in a silvery cover, the foal was born.

A celebration started in Sam's head, but she pushed it aside, being sensible.

Clear the membrane from the foal's nose, eyes, and mouth. That's what the book had said. Sam pulled on rubber gloves, but before she could do anything else, a flurry of sound came from the stall.

She could sort of see through the translucent covering.

Legs thrashed and a little head flung from side to side. Sunny looked back in amazement as slender, black legs kicked and a tiny, slick body bucked on its side.

Ten minutes. The books said the foal might try to stand in ten minutes. This time, the books were wrong.

Free of the silver covering, the storm-born filly struggled to stand.

Now Sam could see her whole body. She had a tiny dished face and huge, luminous eyes. She was satiny black without a speck of white.

Sam realized one of her rubber-gloved hands was

pressed against her chest, but her heart had already gone out to the filly.

She'd never seen anything so wonderful. So beautiful.

Only once, her memory chided.

And then Sam remembered.

The tiny black filly looked just like her father.

Chapter Eight ⌒

With a whinny that came out as a squeak, the foal tried to wobble to her feet but failed.

Sunny blinked at the commotion and stared at the foal beside her. The buckskin gave a low nicker. She looked at Sam, then stared into the corner of her stall.

Sam pressed her lips closed. She'd heard herself breathing hard, as if she'd been running.

Don't panic, she told herself. The books said many mares, especially first-time mothers, felt disoriented following their foal's birth.

Poor Sunny. Just minutes ago she'd been alone in her stall. Now a shiny black stranger kicked out at all angles and made little fussing noises.

When Sunny glanced at her again, Sam decided to disappear.

Mother and foal needed time to bond.

In the wild, Sunny would have gone away from the herd. Together, she and her foal would have learned everything about each other. Forever after, Sunny would have known the scent and shape of the foal she had to protect and the foal would know which mare to count on for food and protection.

Sam squatted next to the stall wall and peered through a narrow gap between two boards.

Exhausted from her struggle to stand, the filly trembled. She looked fragile and defenseless.

Rain hammered the roof. Outside, Sam could see raindrops pelting the ground.

The foal was safe and warm in the barn beside her mother, but how would she have survived outside?

The storm's moisture made the pine boards smell like Christmas as Sam stared into the stall to see Sunny sniff her foal's front hooves, then lick her pasterns, then lick as far as her neck would reach, up to the foal's knobby black knees.

The filly was so lightweight, she moved with the force of her mother's tongue, but she seemed to love the attention. When Sunny scooted closer, head extended, the filly mirrored her movements.

Sunny's golden nose was shaded with black around her nostrils and lips. When she touched her baby's muzzle, neither recoiled in surprise. In the lantern light, it was hard to see where one left off and the other began.

That's how it should be, Sam thought, then wished the thought hadn't crossed her mind. Would she ever stop missing her own mother? She wanted to stop wishing she could say, "Hey Mom, look."

Sunny lowered her head and lipped the filly's front legs, then licked them again. Her head bobbed as she did, then her eyelids drooped, her head nodded, and she slept.

Sam watched the foal survey her surroundings. Her tiny black head was about the size of Sam's fisted hands placed end to end. Her eyelids drooped, but instead of sleeping, the foal's head wobbled down, letting her lips touch the straw. Then her head tilted back, barely supported by her weak neck, to look at the rafters.

Take a nap, Sam told her silently, but the filly didn't. Like her father, she was on the alert.

Wind lashed whips of rain through the barn door. Despite the shelter of her stall, the birth-damp filly shivered.

"Time for a rubdown," Sam whispered.

She unfolded the white towel from her foal kit, careful not to allow a molecule of dirt to touch it.

Dr. Scott had said that after mare and baby had bonded, it was safe to go in and rub the foal dry—if the mare allowed it.

Straightening her knees so slowly she felt like an old woman, Sam stood and looked at Dark Sunshine. The mare's eyes stayed closed.

The foal shivered again and pulled her gangly legs a little closer to her body. If she were too cold, she might stay down, curled up for warmth, instead of standing to nurse. Drying her wet coat would be a good idea.

Sam picked up the bran mash and slid back the bolt on the stall door. She'd use everything she knew about reading the expressions of horses, because she'd seen Sunny with ears pinned back and hatred in her eyes. Tired or not, the mare could wield her teeth and hooves with deadly accuracy.

Sam opened the stall door and slipped inside. She set the bran mash just in front of Sunny. The mare opened her eyes. Though her nostrils quivered at the hearty cereal aroma, she was more interested in Sam.

With weary exasperation, Sunny's expression seemed to ask, "Don't you think I knew you were hiding out there?"

Sam didn't answer, just moved carefully around the edge of the stall.

Never get between a mare and her foal, Dad had told her.

Sam didn't. She kept the foal between them. Even then, Sunny's ears flicked backward. They weren't pinned and her eyes weren't narrowed. Yet.

"You're a good mom, aren't you, Sunny," she crooned to the mare.

The buckskin lay just ahead of the foal nestled at her flank. If the mare stood or made a stronger threat, Sam was determined to run for it.

Rubbing the foal dry was optional, and Sam knew no one would come to her aid if she was injured.

"I promise not to hurt your baby," she said, lowering to her knees, still watching the mare. "You trust me, don't you, girl? I've got to look down to touch her. So, if I do anything you don't like, warn me *before* I get trampled, okay?"

Sam dabbed the soft terry cloth at the foal's eyes and nostrils until they were clean.

The black filly didn't struggle and Sunny didn't protest. After one quiet minute, Sam released the breath she'd been holding. Some books said gentle contact with a foal during its first hour could make it friendlier to humans its whole life long.

"And that means you need to stay with me," Sam whispered as she caressed one satiny ear. "Because if you decide to go hang out with your dad, you'll discover that not all people are kind."

As she rubbed the filly's inky neck, Sam wondered whether the Phantom had come this afternoon not to steal Dark Sunshine but because he knew his foal was about to be born.

This was no time for wondering. She had to focus on Sunny and this tiny horse. No matter how gently she massaged, the foal's little head wobbled. The filly was so delicate.

As Sam stroked her short, smooth back, the foal watched with curiosity, but when Sam touched her flank, instinct reminded the filly she was a mustang.

Twig-thin forelegs stiffened, her head ducked in protest, and she let out a high-pitched squeal that made Sam's ears ring.

Eyes clamped on Sunny, Sam scooted away from the filly. One knee back, then the other, then the first one, until her boot sole hit the side of the stall. Slowly, Sam stood.

Sunny's black-rimmed ears tipped forward. Way forward.

Sam knew she should escape while the mare was still trying to puzzle things out.

Quality time with her new horse could wait.

Sam almost made it to the stall door before Sunny rocked to her feet with a groan.

Sam's hand had already drawn the bolt when Sunny swung her head forward into Sam's shoulder.

"I get it," Sam said. She slipped from the stall and closed the door instead of standing to rub the bump she knew would bruise. "You think it would be a good idea if I visited from outside."

Sam had read that foals saw all large objects as pretty much the same, but as soon as the black filly saw Sunny stand, she seemed to realize she was hungry.

"You know your mama," Sam said.

The filly placed her front hooves far apart and pushed with her back legs, trying to stand.

Her dainty ears flopped out to each side. Sam really hoped they wouldn't stay that way.

Her little whisk of a tail stuck straight up, as if she thought it was a critical part of balance.

Were those long legs supposed to look so rubbery? They seemed to bend at many angles, not just at the joints.

Poor little thing, Sam thought as the foal finally balanced on four trembling legs. Her shiny black muzzle reached toward Sunny, stretching as far as her new neck would allow, but the mare actually moved a step away, to begin eating the bran mash.

"Sunny!" Sam whispered. "That's mean."

Sunny ignored them both and began chewing her bran with pleasure.

Maybe that was the way nature meant the mare to act, because the foal didn't give up. Concentrating as if she were trying to do algebra, the little black filly moved one front leg, then the other, then used a little buck to make her hind legs catch up.

Once, her legs quivered so hard, Sam was sure she'd fall, but the filly's head came up, her ears pointed at her mother, and she swayed forward until she ran into Sunny's side.

Then she turned her head to nurse. Sunny's head lashed around, ears flattened, and her teeth clacked on the air.

Surprised but not discouraged, the filly swayed on her unsteady legs and gave it another try. This time Dark Sunshine let the filly nurse while she went back to the bran mash.

Sam sighed in relief as the filly's tail swished from side to side.

"Looks like it's dinnertime for you two. I'm kind of hungry, myself," Sam said.

She glanced at her watch. It was nine o'clock. No wonder she was hungry. The horses would probably be fine if she ran into the house, grabbed something, and ran back.

She stared at Sunny and her foal, feeling as if she'd forgotten something.

"Tepid water," she said quietly. Dallas had told her the mare would be thirsty after she gave birth, but should be given tepid water because cold water might give her stomach cramps.

Sunny hadn't been nosing around her bucket yet, so Sam guessed she still had time to heat some water and mix it with what the mare already had.

Sam crept away from the stall with Blaze behind her.

"You've sure been quiet," she said, petting his black-and-white head. As they stepped out into the summer night, she knelt and hugged his neck. "Thanks for keeping watch."

Blaze tolerated her hug for a minute, then wagged his tail, wriggled loose and bounded into the ranch yard, barking.

In the ten-acre pasture, Amigo, Popcorn, and Sweetheart reacted by racing in mock terror across the field.

The storm had moved east. Lightning glimmered

over the Calico Mountains. Here, all was quiet except the vines fluttering against the trellis Gram had built in the garden. When they bloomed, they'd be morning glories and scarlet runner beans.

Was it their fresh green smell wafting on the breeze, or Gram's English lavender, Sam wondered as she picked her way toward the dark house.

She'd have to grab the flashlight from on top of the refrigerator as soon as she got inside, but outside the long summer dusk was just ending.

Puddles the size of ponds reflected a blue-gray sky streaked with indigo clouds and sprinkled with stars.

Shining overhead and reflected underfoot, the moon looked like a pearl.

The balmy night and the new life in the barn behind her filled Sam with exhilaration.

The Phantom's foal had been born healthy and beautiful. Sunny had come through the birth, happy and strong.

Sam held her arms out to each side and started to spin. No one was watching as she whirled, turning the ranch into a smear of colors as rainwater splashed her jeans.

She'd stood guard over the horses, helped where she could—and she'd done it all alone. Dark Sunshine trusted her as never before. And the new filly was hers.

Sam spun faster in a dance of wild celebration.

"I did it!" she yelled as Blaze barked at the sky.

She'd worry about her muddy boots tomorrow.

Chapter Nine ❧

The ranch house kitchen was dark and still.

Sam froze before closing the door behind her. Something was moving upstairs.

She quietly lifted the telephone receiver. Still no dial tone, but she hadn't expected any. She'd only hoped for it.

Her elation forgotten, she grabbed the flashlight from the top of the refrigerator. She slid the switch to ON and a golden beam lit the kitchen. Thank goodness Gram always kept it filled with fresh batteries.

Sam started toward the door into the living room, then stopped. Why should she go looking for trouble?

The hermit of Snake Head Peak was mostly harmless, and he'd never been to River Bend Ranch, so she had no reason to think it was him. Flick, the wild horse rustler she'd stolen Dark Sunshine from, was in jail. At least, he was supposed to be.

Sam listened intently. What she heard wasn't footsteps. It was more of a slither. Gram had warned her to watch for snakes in the garden . . .

Suddenly, the sound turned familiar.

Sam pushed open the door and played the flashlight's beam on the staircase. She heard padded paws jumping from one step to another. Cougar passed through the shaft of light, eyes glowing green.

"Meow?" Cougar inquired as he came into the dark kitchen.

"You silly kitty," Sam said, whisking him from the floor and into her arms. "You scared me."

Cougar gave Sam's cheek one rough-tongued lick before he struggled to get down. Sam let him jump from her arms.

He paced in front of the refrigerator.

"I'll get you some milk," she said. "But if the power stays out much longer, it won't be cold."

Sam pushed her soggy hair away from her face as she remembered Gram had left the refrigerator well stocked with food because she wouldn't be there to cook.

If Gram were here, she'd put the food into a cooler so that it wouldn't spoil. Sam groaned. If the power wasn't working, neither was the pump. Whatever water was in the pipes was all she'd get from the well until the power came back on.

Was that her responsibility, too?

"I don't think Mrs. Coley is coming. Hotspot must be foaling," she told Cougar.

The brown-striped cat rubbed his face on the refrigerator, pointing out Sam's tardiness in supplying his milk.

"In a minute," she told him.

Even if they were short on water, she'd use what they had for Dark Sunshine. She just had to heat it a little so that it would be tepid.

Sam ran some water into the teakettle, set it on the burner, and turned a dial. A little blue-gold flame spurted into view, looking cheery in the dark kitchen. At least the gas stove worked when the power was out.

Next, she opened the refrigerator door to get some milk for Cougar, and the lights came on.

"Yay!" she cheered as the cat threaded between her ankles.

Sam switched off the flashlight and put it back on top of the refrigerator. As she poured the milk, she hoped the power would stay on. Being the one in charge was fine, but she only wanted to be in charge of the fun stuff. Like the horses.

As soon as she'd taken the chill off the water, Sam picked up the kettle and a brown paper bag. She'd loaded the bag with some bread, a jar of peanut butter, a knife, and some of Mrs. Coley's cookies.

Blaze crossed from the bunkhouse steps, to fall in at Sam's heels.

"No one home over there?" she asked the dog.

Blaze divided his time between the ranch house and the cowboys' bunkhouse, eating meals in both places, so he was clearly disappointed.

"I forgot to feed you!" Sam said. Blaze usually ate dinner at the same time as everyone else on the ranch. And since she hadn't eaten tonight, she'd forgotten the dog hadn't, either.

She sucked in her breath, feeling guilty, then juggled everything so that she could dig into the sack. She dropped a piece of bread on the ground and tossed him an oatmeal cookie, which he caught in midair.

"A little junk food won't hurt you," she told the dog, and he must have agreed, because he tagged along more closely than before.

As soon as she entered the barn, Sam looked into the box stall.

Lantern light turned the wheat straw pale gold around the horses. Legs folded, head tucked to her chest like a baby bird, the black filly slept beside Sunny.

"It's okay, girl," Sam said when the mare's head jerked up. "I'm giving you a little water."

She could feel Sunny's eyes following her as she tipped the kettle and added water to the bucket.

Before she had time to back away, the mare stood

and drank in great gulps. Sam petted the sweat-stiff hair on the buckskin shoulder. She'd brush Sunny tomorrow, after the mare had rested. Now she'd leave her alone.

Still standing, Sunny watched Sam bring the cot from the tack room and set it up.

When Sam finally sat on it, the mare settled down, too.

She stood foursquare over her foal, each leg a protective post, though her head hung low in weariness.

Sam sat cross-legged on the cot and spread peanut butter on the bumpy whole wheat bread. It was past her bedtime and she should be sleepy, but she wasn't.

It was time to name the filly.

Everyone in her family would have suggestions, but Sam wanted the foal to know who she was now.

If she'd been a registered horse with papers showing her ancestry, the filly probably would have inherited a name.

Let's see, Sam thought. Her mother was Dark Sunshine, her father the Phantom. Or Blackie.

Sam shook her head. She'd been a child when she named the mighty stallion *Blackie*. It had never occurred to her, then, that he'd grow up to be the cloud-white charger she'd seen today. That proved that she needed to think before selecting the filly's name.

Dark Sunshine's parents were wild, so they'd

probably never been named. The Phantom's parents were Princess Kitty and Smoke. Sam turned those names over in her mind.

According to Dallas, Smoke had been part of the Calico Mountain herd, sired by the pacing white stallion who'd lured him into the Black Rock Desert.

A sudden flurry inside the stall told Sam the filly was awake again. Sunny gave a low nicker and Sam peeked into the stall in time to see the foal rise. This time she was up and standing almost at once.

"Good job," Sam whispered.

Testing her legs, the filly kicked out her back hooves and fell.

She was a wild little thing, Sam thought as the filly regained her feet and nudged Sunny.

Frisky and Frolic were good names for a filly, but not for the sleek, swift mare she'd become. Sam liked the sound of Ebony, but she'd learned her lesson about naming a horse for a color that might change.

She could give her a Nevada name like Sage, Tumbleweed, or something that recalled the night she was born.

Hey, yeah, Sam thought.

Stormy? Gale? Whirlwind? Lightning? Thunderclap? Those were better, but still not quite right.

As if in agreement, the filly took a shaky step in Sam's direction, lifted her tiny nose, and whinnied. The effort might have knocked her down, if her tail hadn't been braced against Sunny.

Sam laughed.

"Don't you know mustangs are quiet?" she whispered. "They give signals with their ears. They don't yell."

The black filly gave a snort, then bobbed her head.

"You're sassy, all right," Sam said, and she was reminded of something, maybe something Gram had said, but she wasn't sure what.

She grabbed a cookie from the sack and munched it while the foal had a second dinner.

Sassy didn't suit her.

Lots of noise and excitement in one little place, Gram had said. A tempest in a teapot. And a tempest was a storm.

Sam smiled at the filly.

"What do you think of Tempest?" she asked.

The little horse stared back with matching intensity. Then she wobbled to the other side of her mother and considered Sam past her mother's tail.

Tempest, Sam thought, settling back on the cot. She liked the name just fine. Maybe she'd sleep on it.

Sam woke during the night to the sound of a car passing on the highway. For a second, she thought Mrs. Coley must have finally arrived, though her watch said it was one A.M. She really hoped nothing had gone wrong with Hotspot.

She woke again at two forty-five. This time she heard tiny hooves pelting wood. When she held up the lantern, she saw Tempest had worked herself into a corner of the stall. She butted her head against it until Sunny stood next to her and used her own head to guide the foal back into the middle of the box stall.

Tempest had tried to insist she could get through the corner of the stall through pure stubbornness. *Just like every other creature on this ranch*, Sam thought.

When Sam finally awoke for real, she thought it was because the lantern had gone out and the barn felt cold in the predawn gloom.

All that was true, but when she managed to get her eyes completely open, she realized she'd really awakened because a shadow had fallen over her face.

Someone stood beside the cot, watching her sleep.

Chapter Ten ৩৯

"Darned if you're not floppy as a neck-wrung rooster," chuckled the shadow.

The shadow was no stranger. Only Jake knew how she hated phony Western accents. Only Jake could sneak in while she was sleeping without Blaze biting his leg to the bone. Only Jake would tease her before she was even awake.

But Jake was supposed to be out on the cattle drive, acting as Dad's right hand.

"What are you doing here?" Sam moaned.

She closed her eyes, but it was no use. Her socks and jeans were wet from last night's puddle dance. She felt stiff and clammy.

"Was in the neighborhood," Jake said.

"Funny." Sam squinted up to see Jake's white smile in the dim barn.

"Some girls sit up and open their eyes when people drive twenty miles to see 'em at four o'clock in the morning," Jake said.

Sam sighed so hard, she felt the exhalation through her toes. Maybe she *could* go back to sleep.

Jake gave the cot a kick. It was a very little kick, but Sam wanted to return the gesture. On his shin.

"What do you *want*?" Sam nearly shouted.

"Not a fistfight. I rode Nighthawk last night. It stormed bad. Amazin' electrical storm. Ask Pepper," he urged. "Glad he saw it, 'cause who'd believe lightning could dance on a steer's horns?"

"What?" Sam managed to stand.

"True." Jake raised his hand as if swearing. "Slocum's longhorns got red-eyed and crazy from it, but I don't know why they didn't drop dead."

Stunned by his own out-of-character rambling, Jake closed his mouth and sat on a hay bale. When he yawned, Sam realized he'd been up all night, too, riding circles around a storm-spooked herd of cattle.

She'd be nicer to him if he gave her a chance.

But wait.

Last night. The storm. *Tempest!*

"I must be brain dead!" Sam yelped. She'd seen the horses just a couple of hours ago and they had been fine, but she collided with the side of the box stall in her hurry to check them again.

As she peeked in, she saw Tempest stretch her legs and yawn.

"Jake, did you see?" Sam whispered.

Jake moved to stand beside her, but Sam couldn't take her eyes from the horses.

"Colt or filly?" Jake asked.

Sunny stood and shook the straw from her mane. Instantly, Tempest tried to do the same. She wobbled upright and balanced on her tiny hooves, but when she tried to shake her wispy mane, she fell.

"Filly," Sam said quietly.

After a second try to imitate her mother, Tempest squealed in frustration.

"Her name is Tempest," Sam told Jake, and a sideways glance showed her he was smiling.

"*Temper,* more like," he said.

Jake kept the half smile as he watched, but Sam waited for him to ask how the birth had gone, whether she'd had any trouble, and wasn't she scared doing it all alone.

She tried to blame her fidgeting on her damp jeans and restless night, but Jake knew her too well.

"What's wrong?" he asked. He kept his eyes on the horses while he retied the rawhide strip holding back his black hair. "And don't say 'nothing.'"

"You could say I did a great job for a kid alone," she mumbled, then she looked down, embarrassed by Jake's expression.

"Seems to me the mare did all the work," Jake

said. "Was there trouble?" Jake's hand was on the door bolt, as if he'd go in and check for himself.

There hadn't been trouble. She drew a breath and let it out, wondering why Jake was watching her so intently.

"If you don't want me to, I won't go in. But you don't want that filly turning into a one-person horse."

Sam swallowed hard. In her heart, that was exactly what she wanted. The Phantom was like that, but he was elusive and free. She never knew when she'd see him. Tempest would be with her every day.

"Oh, never mind," Sam said, then touched her hair. When it was as long as Jake's, she'd probably just tie it back, too. Now, she could tell it hadn't dried in its usual smooth curve.

"How bad is it?" she asked when she caught Jake's smirk.

"Kinda like noodles when you boil 'em dry and leave 'em in the pan."

Sam glared at him. If he couldn't be nice, it wouldn't be her fault for snapping back. But she didn't.

Tempest's suckling and the faint grinding of Sunny's teeth against the wheat straw was peaceful.

When she didn't respond to his teasing, Jake gestured toward the house.

"I knocked," Jake said.

He'd settled back into his usual verbal shorthand. From "I knocked," she was supposed to figure out

that Mrs. Coley hadn't answered the door, and neither had Sam, so he'd come down to the barn to see
what was happening.

At least, that's what she thought he'd meant.

"Mrs. Coley never got here," Sam said. Then,
realizing that sounded ominous, she added, "Last I
heard, Hotspot was about to foal and Mrs. Coley
didn't want to leave Ryan on his own because he
seemed kind of nervous."

Darn. Sam could have bitten her tongue. Jake
and Ryan had been rivals since the day they'd met.
She'd just given Jake one more weakness to add to
his list of reasons to scorn Ryan Slocum.

"That so?" Jake pretended not to gloat, but his
tired brown eyes had turned lively. "Brynna told me
she talked to Mrs. Coley and they were fretting over
the chance the road would wash out, but not—what's
that smell? Somethin' on fire?"

After one instant of panic, Sam realized Jake had
caught the chemical scent lingering from the burned
telephone lines.

"Not anymore," she said. "Lightning struck the
telephone line."

Jake had walked out of the barn to stare up at the
damaged pole almost before she finished. His eyes
measured the distance between the barn and the pole.
Maybe now he'd give her credit for what she'd done.

"Have you notified the phone company?" he
asked, walking backward while he stared up, trying

to see how much of the wire was burned, she guessed.

"Well, I would have, but I have this little problem. The phones are out because the lines were on fire."

"Why are you so touchy?" Jake looked mystified.

"It's nothing," Sam said. "I guess I'm just tired."

She watched Jake's expression. If he dared to tell her he'd been up all night, too, she'd scream.

"Let me help you feed," he said, gesturing at the horses and chickens.

"I can do it," she said, because all of a sudden she'd noticed Jake was limping.

Ever since the fall that had broken his leg, he'd been in pain whenever he overstressed the leg or when it rained. He'd never admitted that, of course, but why else would he limp?

Sam scolded herself. *You jerk*. Even though Jake had been up all night, riding in the same conditions that had contributed to his injury, he had come to check on her.

"Thanks for coming by," she said, and though she was only trying to show her appreciation, she saw Jake's face close like a slammed door. He thought she was trying to get rid of him.

"You make me crazy, Jake Ely," she said, and gave him a punch in the arm.

That he understood.

Jake shrugged and gave her a lopsided smile.

"Ground's all turned to slurry, so we're taking the herd across higher ground, through the mountains.

Before we got too far out, I wanted to see that foal. Had a feeling the storm would bring her early."

Sam tilted her head sideways, trying to read Jake like she would a horse, but he hid his feelings too well. Had he come to check on her or to see the foal? She couldn't tell and she figured it didn't matter. In fact, she hoped he'd come to see the foal, because she could take care of herself.

"Better get back now," Jake said, walking toward the faded blue truck he shared with his brothers.

Watching Jake's wide shoulders and faint limp as he moved away, Sam felt instantly lonely.

"I'm going to turn them out in the pasture for the first time," she said. "Want to watch?"

Jake stopped and passed his car keys from one hand to the other.

Blaze bounced to his side, panting in excitement as if he might go for a ride in Jake's truck.

Jake gave the dog an idle pat, then asked, "Dr. Scott been by yet?"

"No one has. Except for you," Sam said.

"That buckskin bein' the way she is, I'd keep her in the stall till the doc's had a chance to check her."

Sam nodded slowly. Sunny was cautious around the vet at any time. Right after foaling, she might be even more leery of him.

Leaving Sunny in the stall, within easy reach of the vet, was a better idea.

Why hadn't it been hers?

Jake shooed Blaze back and pulled open the truck door. Its squeak almost covered his next words.

"But she's your horse," he said.

"That's right!" Sam snapped. Jake didn't say anything, but she saw him stiffen.

On her first day back on the ranch, Dad had told her she'd missed a good chance to keep her mouth closed. She'd missed a lot of chances since then, including now.

She'd always resented Jake bossing her around, but it stung more because of what Dr. Scott had said. Jake was Dad's right hand.

She wasn't.

As Jake backed up the denim-colored truck, Sam waved. He held one hand out the driver's window in response. It wasn't quite a wave, but almost.

What did that mean?

Sam sighed as the truck clunked over the bridge.

Jake wasn't a horse. She shouldn't have to study his outside to figure out what was going on inside his head.

Still, what she'd read in his gesture made her happy. Jake hadn't ignored her wave. That meant he wasn't totally irritated by her jealousy.

"In fact," Sam told Blaze, "I'll bet you a dog cookie he didn't even know I was jealous."

The Border collie ran a circle around her and Sam decided she could take that as agreement.

Chapter Eleven ♋

Sam had fed all the horses, refilled their water troughs, tossed cracked corn and chicken scratch out for the hens, and refilled the lantern with fuel.

Dawn lightened the sky to a hazy coral that promised another hot day and Sam couldn't face it. She knew she'd feel better after she had breakfast, but she'd eaten all the oatmeal cookies the previous night, the thought of peanut butter made her stomach turn, and she didn't have the energy to walk to the house.

Amigo, Sweetheart, and Popcorn called to Sunny, but she didn't answer. In the wild, she would have been far away from her herd, protecting her foal from being stepped on or investigated too enthusiastically.

Sam figured Sunny's silence was her natural yearning to keep her hiding place secret—even if it was just across the ranch yard.

The barn was still cool, so Sam sat on the cot. Head forward, she positioned the heels of her hands to keep her eyelids open.

When Blaze began barking, she didn't even try to guess why.

"Good boy," Sam told him, but Blaze had bounded from the barn.

Past the rooster's crow and the splash of paws in puddles, Sam heard the diesel purr of the blue Mercedes-Benz. Mrs. Coley was back.

Sam felt a little dizzy, but she stood up. Maybe her kind neighbor had brought food.

"Lands, Jake was right."

Dressed in jeans with a blue bandanna tied like a headband around her short gray hair, Mrs. Coley looked a lot peppier than Sam felt.

Together, they shaded their eyes and studied the telephone pole that had burst into flames the night before.

By daylight, Sam saw the black scorch near the top of the pole. It wasn't that far from the barn. If there had been more wind and less rain the previous night, she and the horses could have been in the midst of a disaster.

"When it became clear I wasn't going to get back here at any reasonable hour," Mrs. Coley said, "I tried to call you. Your line was busy, busy, busy. Now I know why." Mrs. Coley looked apologetic. "But I just figured you were talking to a friend. So I thought you were fine—which of course you are."

Mrs. Coley looked so relieved, Sam couldn't wait to show off Tempest.

"Want to come see my new baby?" Sam asked proudly.

"Absolutely," Mrs. Coley said, and she slipped her arm through Sam's for the walk to the barn.

"Did you say something about Jake?" Sam asked while they walked.

"That boy is so responsible, it's hard to believe he's not grown," Mrs. Coley said with an admiring tsk of her tongue. "After he left here, he came by my place and called the phone company and Dr. Scott, then told me all about your new little one."

"I was going to see if I could use your cell phone when you got here," Sam said softly.

Sam knew she was just feeling sorry for herself. Time and again, Dad and Gram and Brynna had told her they were proud of her, that they trusted her. But it never seemed to last.

Just last week they'd congratulated her for finding Daisy, the orphaned yellow calf, but then Brynna had insisted she be tested before she was allowed to ride Popcorn.

". . . your dad was downright sensible to leave the ranch in your care," Mrs. Coley was saying. "You're doing a fine job."

"Thanks," Sam said. She felt herself blush.

So what if Dr. Scott had said Jake was Dad's right hand? She had no reason to complain.

"Tell me about Hotspot's foal," Sam urged as they detoured around the flock of scratching hens.

"He had a tough time coming into this world, but he's a cute little thing. Gorgeous bright bay coat, knee-high stockings in front. I wouldn't be surprised if he develops a nice Appaloosa blanket like his mother."

Sam smiled. Again, she told herself she hadn't really believed that Linc Slocum would give her Hotspot's "mongrel" foal.

"He doesn't look like the hammerhead?"

"No sign of his sire anywhere about him," Mrs. Coley said. "In fact, you remember what a big brute that blue roan was?"

"I do," Sam said. She recalled the horse's huge hooves thudding on the Phantom's ribs and his square teeth clamping on the stallion's white neck during their violent battle. The Phantom had beaten the hammerhead, but it hadn't been easy.

"If anything"—Mrs. Coley lowered her voice and looked around as if someone might overhear—"this little fella is something of a runt."

"But I bet Ryan loves him."

"Oh my, yes. He's got the mare's papers all spread out in Linc's study and he's brought in books of literature, searching for just the right name."

If Ryan had staked his claim on the colt, there was no way Linc Slocum would take him away. It was for the best, Sam supposed, but Tempest and the little Appaloosa would have had a great time charging around together.

As soon as they entered the barn, Sam saw Dark Sunshine holding her head high, staring over the stall wall at Mrs. Coley.

"Is she a good mama?" Mrs. Coley asked quietly. She offered Sunny the back of her hand to sniff, but the buckskin backed away, keeping her body between the humans and her foal.

"The best," Sam said. "And you'll see, if she ever moves, that Tempest is really pretty."

"You must have done everything right," Mrs. Coley said, "because first-time mothers can be spooky. Now, *Tempest*," she repeated. "That's a literary name, too, isn't it?"

"I don't know," Sam said. "Is it?"

"I think so," Mrs. Coley said, tilting her head as she tried to see past Sunny. "It's a play by Shakespeare and I think it starts with a gigantic storm."

"Wow," Sam said. "I was thinking of a tempest in a teapot."

"That's even better," Mrs. Coley said, then she laughed as the black filly tottered past her mother's tail and pretended to stare at the far wall. Tempest's eyes rolled to show the whites and she kicked out her hind legs.

"She didn't fall this time!" Sam said. "She must be getting stronger!"

"And pretty feisty, too," Mrs. Coley said. "I think you're going to want to keep your hands on this one, make sure she doesn't turn wild on you."

Dr. Scott arrived not long after Mrs. Coley had finished feeding Sam pancakes and hot chocolate for breakfast.

The young vet was pleased, overall, but as he stood in the stall examining the horses, he lectured Sam about making sure the mare got plenty to eat and plenty of rest.

"Keep her in her own pen for at least two weeks," he told Sam. "And watch her."

"What's wrong?" Sam asked.

"Nothing serious, but I think she's a little nervous."

"Really? I didn't even have to hold her for you this time."

"I know, but look over there," the vet said, pointing at a place where the wooden stall had been chewed white. "She's been cribbing. It's no big deal, but she hasn't done it before, has she?"

Sam shook her head. She shouldn't have let other people cluster around the stall—not Jake, not Mrs. Coley, nobody.

"Will it make her sick?"

"Unlikely," he said. "It's like biting fingernails is for a person, but it's not a sign we want to ignore.

"Most of the chemical cures that you spread on

the wood to make it taste bad aren't things I want her eating while she's nursing. They'll go into her milk and end up in the foal. Just not a good idea.

"But that's the only bad news," Dr. Scott said. "The foal looks great and Sunny will be fine. Let's do something fun to distract the mare from her worries."

"Okay," Sam agreed.

"So far, the only world this little one knows is her stall. Let's turn them out into the pasture."

"Tell me what to do," Sam said. She slipped into the stall with Dr. Scott and the horses.

"Whoa!" the vet said. Even though she was a small horse, Sunny knocked him from her path as she bolted forward.

Halfway through the stall door, Sam stopped. "What happened?"

Dr. Scott ignored her for a full minute. First he waved his arms, backing the mare away from the door, showing her she was not allowed to knock him around.

Then he soothed the mare with kind words and explanations. Finally he looked up and nodded in Sam's direction.

"She never noticed that before, I'll wager."

"Noticed what? The stall door?" Sam asked. "I've taken her in and out this way. And through from the pasture, too."

Closing and bolting it behind her, Sam stood inside the stall and stared at the door. Nothing had changed.

There were no splinters, no horse hair snagged on a board, nothing that should have startled Sunny.

"I don't see anything, either," the vet assured her. "But she's looking at it differently. Must be because of the foal." He shook his head. "You came into the stall that way last night when you dried off Tempest, right?"

"Yeah," Sam admitted. "But nothing bad happened when I did, so I don't think she's remembering that."

Dr. Scott scratched his head. "So maybe it's not that she realized something could get in." He looked up at Sam, frowning. "Maybe she just discovered she could get out."

The suggestion gave Sam chills.

"I'll keep it bolted," she promised.

Together they haltered Dark Sunshine, then Sam took the lead rope.

"I'll hold Tempest while you go on ahead," the vet said.

Tempest was so small that, even though the filly was standing, Dr. Scott's arms could encircle her from chest to hind legs.

"Why are you holding her back?" Sam asked as she started toward the pasture.

"It's not likely, but just in case Sunny gets out there and starts kicking up her heels, glad to be outta this stall . . ."

"Got it," Sam said.

One kick like that could kill Tempest. Sam bit her lip. She had a lot to learn. She just hoped none of her mistakes cost the horses pain or suffering.

Once the two were freed in the grassy pasture, they didn't run. Tempest stuck to her mother's side as if she were attached with Velcro. Her head just reached Sunny's ribs and it stayed there as the buckskin explored the enclosure, grazing with half-closed eyes.

"Shall I leave them out here?" Sam asked.

"I think so," Dr. Scott said. "They've got shade. Tempest can look across at the other horses, the chickens, and Blaze, learn a little bit about her world."

"Okay," Sam said. "But I'm putting them in before dark."

To Sam, the horses seemed too exposed. She kept picturing the cougars that had prowled the ridge the previous winter. Those particular cats were gone now, but what if more were nearby? She should have asked Jake to check for paw prints.

Fragile and shining like black satin, Tempest stood between Sunny and the fence closest to the ridge trail, where the cougars had come down. An adult cougar could leap the fence.

With nightmarish logic, Sam decided a cougar couldn't carry the foal back over the fence. But she wasn't sure. The big cats were amazing athletes. And someone—Brynna, Jake, or Dad—had told her that colt meat was a cougar's favorite.

"You're shivering like it's January, not June," the vet said. "They're gonna be just fine."

Sam only hoped he was right, because if she'd learned anything living on a ranch, it was that anything could happen.

Chapter Twelve 👁

No monsters came at midnight.

Or two A.M.

Or four.

By the time Mrs. Coley woke Sam at six thirty the next morning, the mare and foal had slept and nursed their way through ten peaceful hours.

For Sam, wearing a pink T-shirt and lightweight sweatpants to sleep on the cot turned out to be more restful than the soggy socks and jeans she'd worn the night before.

Instead of waking to a shadow lurking above her as she had yesterday, Sam awoke to a whisper.

"Buttermilk donuts."

Mrs. Coley was standing nearby holding a white

saucer and a blue mug.

"What?" Sam sat up so quickly, the cot wiggled, and Mrs. Coley had to step back.

She didn't move so far away, though, that Sam couldn't see the tender pastry circles with wisps of steam rising toward the barn rafters.

"If you're a ranch woman," Sam said, yawning, "are you required to be a good cook?"

"It helps," Mrs. Coley said, seating herself on a hay bale.

"What if you want to spend all your time working with horses and cattle and stuff like that instead?"

"You've still got to eat," Mrs. Coley said. "Good thing about cooking is you're forced to practice every day. And the more thought you put into it, the better it tastes. Grace told me you've made a pretty good start on lasagna."

Sam smiled, took a donut, and bit into it.

"Yummy," she said, but she was thinking that Mrs. Coley might be right. Maybe she could do both, like her mother had.

"Your mare was my inspiration for the donuts," Mrs. Coley said.

Sam laughed, confused.

"When I was a little girl, my favorite television show starred Roy Rogers and Dale Evans—the queen of the cowgirls," Mrs. Coley explained. "Dale wore a fancy fringed leather skirt and rode a buckskin horse named Buttermilk."

"Queen of the Cowgirls" was a title she wouldn't mind having, Sam thought, but she'd have to earn it after breakfast.

Sam took the blue mug, sipped, then licked a powdered-sugar-and-cocoa mustache from her lips.

"Thank heavens for Dale Evans," she said with a sigh.

"You're certainly a lot more chipper than you were yesterday," Mrs. Coley said. "Think you can handle the day alone?"

"Of course!" Sam said. A night's sleep had calmed her worries over cougars in the yard and prowlers in the house.

"I need to get back to the Gold Dust," Mrs. Coley said. "Ryan surely would have called if he was concerned about the colt, but there was another little problem brewing yesterday and I'd like to be there to head it off."

"Something to do with the horses?" Sam asked.

"Nothing like that," Mrs. Coley said. "Rachel is bored."

Sam wasn't surprised. The most popular girl at Darton High School probably felt neglected after a week of summer vacation. Without fans to fawn over her, Rachel would crave some other kind of entertainment. And her daddy wasn't there to give it to her.

"Gram always says if you can't say something nice, don't say anything at all," Sam reminded herself out loud.

"She's right, of course," Mrs. Coley said. "And I do try to remember it's not entirely her fault that she is who she is. It's a matter of upbringing."

Sam wasn't so sure. She thought of her first days at Darton High School. Rachel had purposely broken a camera with which Sam had been entrusted, then let Sam take the blame.

"Maybe," Sam said.

Even if she'd been given everything she ever wanted, Sam didn't think she'd be that mean. Or that stuck-up. Rachel really believed expensive clothes, high-maintenance hair, and loads of money made her better than others.

"Since Linc's not there to drive her to Reno for a manicure and since I have other work, Rachel's harassing Ryan something awful."

"Even she should understand that a baby animal needs looking after," Sam said.

"You'd think that would be the case," Mrs. Coley agreed.

"Ryan will stay with Hotspot and the foal," Sam said, but she wasn't sure she was right.

Ryan was a nice guy, and handsome. Raised in England by his mother, he was smart, polite, and not nearly as stuck-up as his sister.

Jen had a serious crush on Ryan, but Sam wondered if he really liked Jen or if he was just going along with her. Sometimes it seemed Ryan lacked what Dad called "backbone."

For example, he'd hidden Golden Rose, the long-lost Kenworthy palomino, when he knew she must belong to someone else.

Ryan had never thought of training a mustang to race in the Superbowl of Horsemanship, either. But when he heard Jake planned to gentle a pinto running wild on tribal lands, Ryan had suddenly jumped at the idea. He'd talked Mrs. Allen into letting him train Roman, one of the mustangs from her wild horse sanctuary.

On the other hand, Ryan had spotted Tinkerbell's natural jumping talent, and that had helped give the draft horse a better life.

Ryan wasn't exactly dishonest, but would he have the guts to stand up to Rachel? Eventually his twin might wear him down and convince him it was safe to leave the new colt alone.

"I'll be fine without you, but I think you're right. Ryan could use someone else on his side," Sam said.

"All right, then," Mrs. Coley said. "I'll leave my cell phone here for you—"

"You don't have to," Sam began, but Mrs. Coley made a dismissing motion with her hands, so Sam didn't argue.

"And you've had your talk with Dr. Scott," Mrs. Coley went on, "so you know what today will be like?"

"He said mostly eating and sleeping for the horses," Sam told her.

"Plenty of both," Mrs. Coley agreed. She stood

next to the box stall and watched the mare and foal. "That little Tempest will want to be fed two or three times every hour. Poor Sunshine," Mrs. Coley said, clucking her tongue as the mare sized her up, then blew through her lips, dismissing her as a threat.

A breeze blew in from outside. It smelled like rain.

"Are we supposed to get another storm?" Sam asked.

The early morning air was so warm that Sam wanted to replace her sweatpants with shorts, but high desert weather changed quickly.

"I really couldn't tell you, Samantha." Mrs. Coley looked surprised at herself. "I've been so busy, I haven't had time to turn around, let alone listen to a weather report. I'll tell you what, though—when the telephone repair folks come out, ask them. If there's anyone who keeps an eye on the weather as much as a rancher, it's folks who climb electrified poles for a living!"

Overnight, Tempest had learned how to manage her legs. She bounced around the stall as if her black hooves were spring-loaded. When Sam turned the pair into the pasture, Tempest recognized it as her playground.

Sunny moved to the highest spot in the pasture. The small knoll was dry, though the rest of the enclosure had its share of marshy spots and puddles.

Instead of sticking to her mother's side as she had the day before, Tempest ran a loose circle around Sunny, then stopped. With her fluffy mane stirring in the breeze, the filly looked over her world.

Sam could almost hear Tempest thinking. Nothing bad had happened while she was running. And it had been fun.

She did it again. And again, then flopped down on the dewy grass to nap.

Sam went back into the barn to change the bedding in the box stall. It only took a few minutes, but by the time she looked into the pasture, Tempest was up and running again.

She was born with mustang memories, Sam thought. They told her that strong legs were the key to a long life.

Sweetheart neighed from across the ranch yard and Tempest dashed off, splashing through puddles as she taunted the old pinto to run after her. Soon the horses in the ten-acre pasture were running, too, and Sam wished, again, that Hotspot's foal was here to play chase with the black filly.

The fence line closest to the ridge trail must have been a little lower than the rest of the pasture, because the biggest puddles were there.

Black brush of a tail raised high, Tempest pranced over to one of the puddles, reared back on her hind legs, then rocked down, making a splash.

Dark Sunshine raised her head. Blades of grass

still clung to her lips as she trotted toward her baby. She restrained the filly with her nose, keeping her back from the slickest, deepest part of the puddle.

If a newborn horse could pout, Tempest did. Planting each hoof with her new power, she stomped back to the middle of the pasture and flung herself down for another nap.

The day went on that way and by late afternoon, Tempest had taught herself to jump. Tail high, she'd run a few circles around Sunny, then head off for a puddle.

Sam had never noticed that Sunny was shy of water, but she tried, time and again, to keep Tempest from running through it.

The filly defied her mother, leaping and clearing everything. When the barn's shadow darkened one section of grass, Tempest even tried to jump that.

In spite of her day of grazing, Sunny looked gaunt. It wasn't that she'd lost weight, exactly, but the mare's eyes looked sunken and anxious.

I'm probably making this up, Sam thought. She leaned against the fence, staring at the pair of horses. She ran her fingers across the top rail, back and forth.

She didn't want to call Dr. Scott and confess that Sunny looked even more nervous than yesterday. He'd been pleased with the care she'd given the horses and she didn't want to shatter his image of her.

She pushed off from the fence and walked toward

the house. She could feed Blaze his dinner, then decide about calling anyone.

As soon as she saw Mrs. Coley's cell phone sitting on the kitchen table, she called Gold Dust Ranch. Mrs. Coley would offer advice, but she wouldn't be condescending about it.

"Hello!"

Sam held the phone away from her ear. The lilting British accent was Rachel's and she sounded mad.

"Hi," Sam said. "It's Samantha Forster." She hated the fact that her own voice sounded hesitant, so she cleared her throat and tried again. "If Mrs. Coley's there, I'd like to speak with her."

"So would I," Rachel snapped. "I'd like to have a nice long conversation with her about her *duties*, while she drives me into town for a very important appointment. She, however, would rather muck about in the—" Rachel stopped suddenly her voice turned silky. "Samantha, I know you don't drive, but your friend, Jake Ely . . . ?"

"Yes," Sam said through her teeth.

"Has he taken himself off on this cow run?"

Sam smothered her laugh, but barely. "Cattle drive?"

"Whatever. . . ."

"Yes, Jake is on the cattle drive."

"Truly, why did I expect anything different?" Rachel asked under her breath. "He's never seemed entirely civilized."

Sam tried to think of a single reason to be nice to Rachel. At first she couldn't, but then it occurred to her that someone had to tell Mrs. Coley she'd called.

"I'm sorry, Rachel," Sam said, though she thought her tongue might shrivel up from lying. "But with both mares foaling, it's keeping us all pretty busy."

"Don't I know it," Rachel replied, but then she seemed to remember she was talking to an inferior. "Was there something I could help you with, Samantha? Certainly you didn't call to chat."

Should she leave a message? Sam looked down at Blaze as if he could answer. His tail thumped the kitchen floor.

"Please tell Mrs. Coley I'd like to ask her a question about Dark Sunshine." Sam decided to keep it short. There was no way Rachel could mess up a message of so few words, was there?

"Pardon me? Surely I misunderstood you. Why would you call our housekeeper about the weather?"

The weather? Then Rachel's response clicked. Of course, she'd probably never heard of Dark Sunshine.

"You did misunderstand," Sam began, but when she heard Rachel's insulted indrawn breath, she hurried. "Dark Sunshine is the name of a horse."

During Rachel's few speechless moments, Sam heard the bass throbbing of a sound system. She pictured Rachel in her bedroom suite and knew there was probably no chance the rich girl would call Mrs. Coley to the phone.

"A horse. That's even more amusing." Rachel chuckled. "The little cowgirl is admitting she doesn't know everything there is to know about horses. I'm shocked."

Sam felt her cheeks heat with a blush. That was really stupid, too. She didn't care what Rachel thought of her.

Sam pictured herself throwing the cell phone across the room. If she could be sure it would make a deafening squawk in Rachel's ear, it might be worth it. But since it wasn't her telephone, she just tightened her grip.

"Never mind," Sam said. Why had she even called?

She was about to press the phone's disconnect button when Rachel gave a sigh so heavy, Sam thought she should have felt its gust.

Then, sounding totally put-upon, Rachel continued. "It would really be only a minor inconvenience to transfer your call to the stable phone," Rachel said. "After all, if it means saving a dumb animal from your incompetence, how can I say no?"

Chapter Thirteen ∽

Sam gripped the cell phone more tightly, took a deep breath, and concentrated on the view through the front window. Splashed above the Calico Mountains, she saw a royal blue sky stamped with storybook white clouds.

"Samantha, are you there?"

"Sure," Sam said, proud she hadn't told Rachel her opinion on who was really the dumb animal. "Transferring me to the stable would be great."

Mrs. Coley wasn't concerned about Sunny's nerves, even when Sam told her about the cribbing.

"Mares are exhausted after carrying all that extra weight around for months. When their foals are lively, it can wear them out."

"Okay," Sam said. She frowned at Blaze as he scratched at the kitchen door.

"You just came in," she mouthed at him, but the Border collie ignored her.

". . . sound a little skeptical, Sam, and I don't blame you," Mrs. Coley was saying. "I also trust your instincts. Why don't you go out and examine her yourself? I'm sure you won't find anything, but it may even calm her."

Sam noticed she was nodding as she asked, "Should I just run my hands over her like Dr. Scott does?"

"Brushing her would be better," Mrs. Coley suggested. "She expects that from you."

"Got it," Sam said. She wanted to get out there now. Besides, Blaze had started digging at the bottom of the kitchen door. If he scratched the white paint, Gram would notice.

Using her shoulder to clamp the phone to her ear, Sam used both hands to give Blaze a push away from the door.

"One more thing, Sam," Mrs. Coley said. "Be very careful. You're on your own there. If you let yourself get hurt, you won't be any good to those horses."

Suddenly Blaze broke into a yodeling bark.

"I understand," Sam said, raising her voice. "See you later."

"Yes, you will," Mrs. Coley assured her. "But what's wrong with that dog?"

"He just wants to go out," Sam said impatiently.

"Is someone coming? Don't hang up until you check." Mrs. Coley sounded just like Gram.

Sam pulled back the curtain on the front window, then felt a twinge of guilt.

"Sorry, Blaze," she apologized to the panting dog. Not only hadn't she believed him, but now she was going to lock him inside. "Mrs. Coley? The telephone company people are here. I guess I'd better go show them the damage."

Any other day, Sam would have stopped to watch the woman rising up the telephone pole. Ponytail swinging, equipment strapped around her waist clanking, she jabbed the spiked soles of her boots into the pole as she climbed.

But it wasn't a normal day. While Blaze barked like crazy from inside the house, Sunny decided this intruder could be dangerous.

Teeth bared and ears flattened, Sunny tried to herd Tempest away from the strange, climbing creature. When the mischievous foal tried to dart past to see what was happening, Sunny's teeth clacked in warning.

Convinced by the near-miss to stay back, Tempest stood just behind her mother, watching her stand guard.

Sam eased open the outside gate. Maybe she should start brushing Sunny now. Often the mare relaxed into the grooming as if she were being massaged.

Not this time.

Sunny whirled to face Sam and the danger in the buckskin's body language would have been clear to anyone.

As soon as Sam withdrew and bolted the gate, Sunny advanced toward the telephone pole.

Head high, ears pricked forward, Sunny crossed to the middle of the pasture. Even when she stopped, her legs were poised to charge.

When the repairperson kept climbing upward, Sunny seemed convinced her warning had been heeded. Herding Tempest in front of her, the mare returned to the box stall.

Sam didn't recall leaving it open, but she must have. She needed to pay closer attention. Sunny had escaped from River Bend Ranch once, during the fire last October, and she probably remembered. If something scarier than a pole climber appeared, she might make a break for freedom again.

Even though bolting both stall doors made Sam a little jumpy, she did it. If Sunny came after her, she might have time to climb out of reach.

Although Sunny calmed in the safety of her stall, Sam still haltered and tied her.

It wasn't necessary. As soon as Tempest rested in the straw, Sunny's head drooped and her ears flopped sideways. Her right hind hoof rested on its tip as she waited for Sam to groom her.

"That's better, isn't it, girl?"

The hot weather, combined with the stress of birth, meant that Sunny was shedding. Big time. Before Sam had finished going over the mare, both the air and the body brush were full of buckskin hair.

Sam brushed the mare's chest delicately. Faint scars remained from the night last fall when she'd battered against the round pen, trying to flee the fire.

What a nightmare, Sam thought. She remembered turning all the horses free from the ten-acre pasture so they could escape the flames. But Dark Sunshine had been in the round pen. By the time she heard the mare's screams over the sound of the sirens, Sunny had been panicked, unaware she'd cut her chest trying to break down a round pen made to hold mustangs.

Sunny's skin shivered as if shaking off a fly, and she took a step back when a voice shattered her serenity.

"All done!" shouted the telephone repairperson from outside. "You're back in business."

"Thanks," Sam called quietly.

She wanted to shout out a question about the weather as Mrs. Coley had suggested. She wanted to go out and say thank you and good-bye, too. But her first priority was Sunny. She had to keep the mare calm, so she just listened as the truck drove away.

As it did, Sam realized she didn't know exactly what she was checking for on Sunny's body. Still, she hadn't found any bumps or abnormalities so far.

"How about if I just skip your tummy and flank this time?" she asked, when she was about done.

Sunny was often ticklish. Since she was feeling short tempered and Tempest was sleeping within range of Sunny's hooves, Sam wouldn't take a chance on the foal being accidentally kicked or trampled.

Finally Sam untied the lead rope and slipped the mare's halter off. She rubbed behind Sunny's ears where the headstall had left a sweat mark.

For an instant, Sam thought that was what caused Sunny to wheel. Sam barely had time to get out of her way and flatten herself against the front of the stall.

As Sunny darted toward the door to the pasture, she hopped over Tempest as the foal became aware of her mother's alarm and bolted to her feet.

Nothing she could do would work to calm the mare, so Sam edged toward the fence and began climbing. There was no way she'd take a chance of opening that gate. Sunny could push right past her.

Sam made it over the side of the box stall without the mare paying any attention.

Wide-eyed, the mare listened. Sam couldn't hear anything. Was Sunny fearful, threatening, or just protective of her foal?

Sam left the barn and stood outside in the quiet ranch yard, searching for whatever had attracted the mare's attention.

The white stallion drew her eyes like a magnet.

With eager hoofbeats, the Phantom descended the hillside. Neck arched, tail held high, he nickered, acting like the pet she'd known years ago.

But he wasn't safe here, and he could be a danger to Tempest. She had to make him go.

Sam stayed still. The stallion's pricked ears told her he was curious. If she called his name or welcomed him, the Phantom would come to her.

Even though he was nearly a mile away, Sam heard him snort.

From Ace, that sound usually meant "hi" or "look at me." With the Phantom, it was hard to tell.

Did Sunny hear him? Sam didn't know, but hooves struck the inside of the box stall.

"No!" she shouted. If Sunny broke out, the stall would be ruined, which would be a disaster.

Sam doubted she could fix it well enough to hold the horses again. Worse than that, Sunny would have learned she could break out.

Neither the Phantom nor Sunny took her shout as a threat. Sunny neighed from inside the barn and the saddle horses joined in.

Sweetheart, already agitated by Tempest, raced up and down the fence, hooves thundering like Sam had never heard them before.

The Phantom started down the trail. Was the lure of two mares — Sunny and Sweetheart — too great for him to resist?

I have to stop him, Sam told herself.

Her brain agreed, but her heart remembered how hard she'd worked to regain his trust after his imprisonment by Karla Starr. They'd come a long way since then. The stallion had allowed her to ride him.

Slam! Was that the sound of Sunny's hooves? Stallions could be dangerous to foals. Didn't the buckskin know that?

Or were Sunny's neighs angry, meant to drive him away?

"You can't stay!" Sam shouted. She grabbed the lead rope she'd draped over the fence earlier. Spinning it, she skirted the small pasture and started up the ridge trail.

Confused, the Phantom turned his head to one side.

If he'd charged her back, Sam would have welcomed it. If he'd shied and bolted in surprise, that would have been all right. But the mighty stallion was bewildered.

The trail before her turned hazy. She blinked back her tears, but still tripped on the uneven footing and rocks as she ran up the trail.

Don't be stupid, she told herself. *There's nothing to cry about. You're doing the right thing for him, for Sunny, for Tempest.*

By the time she stopped to rub the back of her forearm across her eyes, the Phantom was gone.

The only movement on the trail was ruby-barked

mountain mahogany, still waving from the mustang's passing.

Only as she trudged back to the barn did she realize why her chest ached. Why, if she'd done what was best for the horses, did it feel like the worst thing for her?

Chapter Fourteen ❧

It wasn't easy keeping a secret that felt like it might break your heart, but Sam did it.

There was no point in telling Mrs. Coley that the Phantom had returned to the ridge, Sam decided as she sat at the kitchen table sharing the tuna casserole and salad Mrs. Coley had made for them. It would only make the stallion a suspect if any domestic mares escaped to join wild herds.

So Sam didn't mention that she'd purposely spooked the wild horse she'd taught to trust her.

When Mrs. Coley walked out to the barn with Sam after they'd finished the dishes, Sam's worry only got worse.

She'd been telling Mrs. Coley about Sunny's

reaction to the telephone repairperson, and they'd decided to pamper the mare with fresh carrots and a rubdown.

Sunny greeted them with narrowed eyes and flattened ears, then rushed toward them until she crashed into the stall wall.

Mrs. Coley took a deep breath and studied the mare.

"Coddling her might be a bad idea," Mrs. Coley said. "We should probably just leave them alone."

Sam crossed her arms tightly at her waist, watching as Tempest ducked Sunny's swishing tail, then tried to position herself to nurse. The mare was definitely nervous. She needed time alone with her foal.

"I think you're right," Sam agreed.

As they turned to leave the barn, Sam was planning how she'd sneak back in to sleep on the cot again tonight. Before they were in the ranch yard, Tempest squealed in pain.

Sam rushed back to the stall. At once, she saw the damp spot on the foal's satiny neck. "Sunny bit her!"

"At least she didn't break the skin," Mrs. Coley muttered, but she was frowning.

"What should we . . . ?"

"Give me a minute," Mrs. Coley said, watching Sunny use her black-shaded nose to knock Tempest away.

"The mare won't let her nurse. We can't have that," Mrs. Coley said. "Is that her green halter?"

"Yes," Sam said faintly. "I don't remember where I left the lead rope, but I'll get another one. Dad told me what to do."

Sam just hoped they didn't have to use the twitch.

In minutes, Sam and Mrs. Coley stood inside the stall. Sam guessed it was a good thing that Sunny seemed more intimidated than angry as she slipped the halter on.

Holding one hand right beneath the buckskin's chin, Sam faced Sunny toward her feed bin. For balance, Sam braced her feet apart, then watched while Mrs. Coley encircled Tempest's body with her arms. She did it just as Dr. Scott had, so maybe Tempest wasn't too frightened. Then Mrs. Coley stood between Tempest and Sunny, protecting the foal from a sudden charge.

"Hold on tight, Samantha," Mrs. Coley said as she glanced over her shoulder. "There'll be no more oatmeal cookies for you if she takes a chunk out of my back."

"I've got a pretty good grip on her," Sam promised. "But poor Tempest. I'd feel better if she cried like a baby."

The filly's spirit seemed to have drained away.

Struck by her mother, held helpless by a strange human, she trembled on unsteady legs, afraid to step close enough to eat. When Mrs. Coley grimaced with effort and lifted her nearer, the filly raised her head, showing her smooth throat while her nose pointed at the rafters.

"Look here, ladies," Mrs. Coley said, frustrated. "This just won't do."

Mrs. Coley sounded a little rough. She talked to Sunny and Tempest as she would to any stubborn animals. Sam tried not to blame her.

"Your baby loves you, Sunny," Sam said, smoothing the buckskin's black forelock away from her eyes. "Why are you acting like this?"

"She can't help it, I guess," Mrs. Coley said. Then, as Tempest cautiously lowered her black nose to drink, "There you go, little one."

Sunny kicked out once, directly behind her, but that was all. After that she stood staring past Sam, as if she wished she were somewhere else while the foal nursed noisily.

From the instant Sunny had come home to River Bend Ranch, Sam had taken responsibility for her. Now, the feeling of guilt built up in Sam's chest until she felt it might pop.

"What am I doing wrong?" she asked Mrs. Coley. "I feel like I'm doing everything Dad and Dallas and Dr. Scott and the books have told me to do, but I must have skipped something."

"It's probably not you," Mrs. Coley said.

"Jake told me that if Tempest's not going to run wild, I should let other people be around her," Sam confessed.

"He told me I was trying to make her like me and no one else."

Sam had such a hard time repeating Jake's

accusation that she was surprised at Mrs. Coley's reaction.

"She's not Jake's horse. He hasn't been around Sunny as much as you have."

When Mrs. Coley met her eyes, Sam had to remind herself to close her mouth. She was that surprised.

"All I'm saying," Mrs. Coley continued, "is this: Go ahead and listen to advice, but when it comes down to it, pay attention to your horse."

"But I thought I was, and—"

Mrs. Coley put her hand on Sam's arm to stop her.

"Sam, we can't read horses' minds. If we could, we'd all be riding in the Olympics or winning the Kentucky Derby."

Mrs. Coley was right, and her observation made Sam feel better. As they waited around to see how the pair went on, Sam turned on the overhead lights and showed the older woman the improvements Dad had made to the barn.

"I guess I don't have to ask the identity of your mascot," Mrs. Coley said. She smiled at the white wooden horse on the door beam.

Sam had forgotten all about Dallas's carving, but seeing it made her smile, too.

"Dallas put him there for luck," she said. "I guess it's working pretty well so far."

"I don't much believe in luck so much as hard work," Mrs. Coley said. "And I'd say these horses have you to thank for all the good that's come to them so far."

Seeing Sam's embarrassment, Mrs. Coley went back to admiring the overhead lights, but agreed with Sam that the mare and foal would probably feel more at ease in the soft glow of the lantern.

"I'll plan on spending the night," Mrs. Coley said when she saw Sam yawn. "It'll be easier with two of us if we end up having to hold her for every feeding." Mrs. Coley held her head in comic despair and laughed. "Did you know it's not unheard of for a foal to drink *fifteen* times an hour during the first week after birth? We could be mighty tired by daybreak."

They stayed in the barn until Tempest moved toward her mother with wary steps.

Poor baby, Sam thought, but Sunny let Tempest nurse as if the bite had never happened.

Sam threw up her hands in puzzlement and Mrs. Coley shook her head.

"That's a good sign, but we can't count on it. Let's see what your dad's got in the tack room."

Instinctively Sam knew what Mrs. Coley wanted to find.

"If you're looking for powdered formula, it's probably in the house," Sam said, sighing. "That's where the calf formula is, anyway."

"Wait!" Mrs. Coley grinned as if she'd had a revelation. "We've got a better solution than that. A hundred times better!"

"We do?"

"Hotspot," Mrs. Coley said. "The birth was tough, but that little blue blood is proving to be a good mother. And her undersized colt hardly eats anything at all. If Sunny won't feed her baby, it's possible Hotspot could take on twins.

"I'm not promising, mind you, but once when I was a girl, we had a mare who did. If I can just remember the way of it. . . ." Mrs. Coley's expression turned thoughtful.

Sam hated the idea. She also knew that she was being ridiculously selfish.

"That is a good solution," Sam managed, but Mrs. Coley wasn't fooled.

"I know it's not what you want," Mrs. Coley said. "Having the foal over at Gold Dust instead of right here where you can see, hear, and touch her isn't the same."

"It's not," Sam said. "But it's a lot better than losing her."

Why did everything have to be so hard? Once Tempest was born, Sam had thought the tough part was over. How could it have turned out to be the easy part?

Jealousy was ugly. Sam felt her face flush as she imagined Ryan Slocum raising the Phantom's filly.

Tempest's third night alive was a tense one for Sam. They left the overhead lights on after all and Sam slept with Mrs. Coley's cell phone, ready to call the kitchen telephone if Sunny turned mean again. She and Mrs. Coley had decided that would be quicker than Sam running to the house for help.

Every time she heard the rustle of straw, Sam jolted upright on the cot and stared into the half darkness. But the horses did fine together: dozing, waking to nurse, then sleeping again.

By morning Sam was a wreck, but the horses pranced into their pasture and played together.

Despite low-hanging clouds in every shade of gray, Sunny and Tempest knew that it was summer and they rejoiced in it. Sunny kept her strides short and Tempest stretched her legs as far as they'd reach as they circled the pasture at a walk, trot, and canter, like show horses.

Then, when her mother fell to grazing, Tempest taught herself to pull Sunny's tail.

At first, Sam gasped. What if Sunny kicked Tempest's delicate black face?

But she didn't. Sunny only moved off a step each time her filly tormented her.

"The little imp!" Mrs. Coley said, then shrugged. "If she'll put up with that, Sunny must be over her crankiness, so I'll tell you what."

"What?" Sam asked.

"I'm going home for a nap."

"And to rescue Ryan from his evil sister?"

A far-off rumble of thunder underlined her words

and Sam slapped a hand over her lips.

"Well," she said, clearing her throat. "That wasn't very nice."

"No, but I do value honesty," Mrs. Coley said. "So I won't pass that along to your gram."

After Mrs. Coley left, Sam felt a little lonely for everyone on the cattle drive. They'd probably had their breakfast of biscuits and gravy hours ago. By now Gram had washed the dishes, broken camp, and moved on.

Dad and Luke Ely were probably riding point, at the front of a thousand cows and calves. Jake, his brothers, the cowboys, and Jen would be ranged along the sides of the big herd unless they were riding drag at the very back.

On her first and only cattle drive, Sam had discovered she liked riding in that solitary position. In spite of the dustiness, she could look at the sky, at tiny wildflowers growing through a crack in the playa, and daydream.

Cattle that had been gathered from all over the range would probably reach the higher summer pastures in a day or two if the improved weather held and Linc Slocum didn't slow them down with some scheme.

Sam stared toward the Calico Mountains. Someone who didn't know her would think it odd that she missed Ace. And Jake, but she didn't exactly miss him. She felt guilty.

Crossing her fingers, Sam hoped Jake had forgotten the bratty remarks she'd thrown at him when he'd driven out to check on her.

Why had she resisted when Jake suggested she keep Sunny in her stall until Dr. Scott had had a chance to check her? It was good advice. All the books said so. But when he'd seen her reluctance and said, *She's your horse*, she'd snapped *That's right!* like a little kid.

Worse than that, when he'd offered to help feed the animals, she'd boasted, *I can do it myself*.

Sam groaned at her childishness. Maybe he'd be too busy to remember. She hoped so, because if she needed Jake's help for anything soon, she was certain he'd enjoy reminding her.

Tempest's thudding hooves drew Sam's attention back to the small pasture. What she saw made her admire Sunny's patience more than ever.

Maybe it was the Phantom's kingly blood running through her veins that made tiny Tempest rear up to paw at her mother's back. Sam had seen young stallions in bachelor herds do that, proving dominance, but how could Tempest be telling her mother that *she* was the boss?

Embarrassed even though no one was eavesdropping on her thoughts, Sam remembered how she'd told Brynna what she wanted her to do this week. But that was different.

Sunny gave a low nicker, stepped beyond her

daughter's pawing hooves, and continued with the business of grazing.

"It's going to be a much better day than yesterday," Sam told Blaze as the dog raised his head up under her hand for a pet.

Sam smoothed her hand over Blaze's back again and again, thinking she might saddle up Popcorn for a ride down to the river.

If Tempest and Sunny kept doing well, she might even pack a picnic lunch and a book, then spend a quiet hour reading while minnows nibbled at her toes.

Sam sighed, feeling limp with relaxation.

But Blaze growled. The fur beneath her hand stood up in warning and Sam closed her eyes. She didn't want to turn around and see who was driving over the cattle guard into River Bend Ranch.

Chapter Fifteen ❧

Rachel Slocum swung her legs out of the passenger seat of the Mercedes. Her high-heeled sandals were a basket weave of thin powder blue straps completely unsuited for a ranch, but they matched her short leather skirt, handbag, and, of course, the car.

"Just a few minutes," Rachel cautioned her twin before he even got out of the driver's side. "You promised."

Coffee-colored curls cascaded over Rachel's shoulders and her hands perched on her hips as she surveyed River Bend Ranch. As she took in the barn and bunkhouse, corrals and pastures and the white, two-story ranch house, her lip curled in disgust.

Sam was instantly defensive. River Bend was a

real working ranch, not a hobby. Dad and Gram had labored for years to keep the cattle operation afloat. They didn't have thousands of extra dollars to spend on landscaping pastures or architecturally beautiful barns.

What was Ryan thinking to just drop in? And especially with Rachel?

Ryan had rolled back the cuffs of his tailored blue shirt. His own dark hair was mussed and when he tried to laugh at his bossy twin, his eyes showed no amusement.

With a start, Sam realized his expression reminded her of Sunny's yesterday. Ryan had had enough of his sister.

The prospect of Rachel coming up against her brother's anger made Sam happy. She shushed Blaze and went out to greet the twins.

"Hi," Sam said, "did you come to see my new baby?"

"I can hardly wait," Ryan said, as his eyes scanned the ranch.

"But we can't stay," Rachel repeated. Tilting her head to one side, she addressed Sam in an accusing voice, "I wanted to be at the mall when it opened, and we're already going to be late."

"Are you going in to Crane Crossing?" Sam asked, making an effort to be polite.

"Unfortunately, yes," Rachel replied. "My nail stylist is in Reno, not Darton, but I'm making the best of what this backwater has to offer. All because my brother, my *twin*, places a horse above me."

"She's wounded to the quick," Ryan said. He strode beside Sam, leaving his sister to pick her way after them. "But only because she's chipped a fake fingernail and needs to have it replaced."

"She's lucky to have a helpful brother," Sam said.

"Don't forget to get the phone, Ryan," Rachel called after them. "And—oh, please! Get this beast away."

Sam turned to see Blaze advancing on Rachel. He wagged his tail at half-mast, willing to give her the benefit of the doubt, but barely.

"There's *saliva* on his mouth," Rachel squealed. "Is he, like, rabid or something? This skirt is suede. He could ruin it. Samantha, call him off!"

"Here, Blaze," Sam said. She patted her leg and the dog returned, but grudgingly. When he kept watching Rachel, Sam thought it showed good judgment.

"Here's Tempest," she said as they reached the pasture.

"What a little beauty!" Ryan watched the black filly run a lap of her enclosure. Fluffy tail straight up in the air, she showed off her newly discovered speed.

Sunny swished her tail and stared suspiciously at the unfamiliar face peering over the fence rails. The mare tossed her head. The corners of her lips curved downward in what really looked like a frown.

Tempest cavorted in front of her mother, bumping

against her front legs, trying to draw her attention. Sunny's attention stayed focused on Ryan.

Telling Ryan she'd be right back, Sam ducked toward the barn.

"I've just got to check the bolts," she said. "Sunny might get excited when she sees strangers, and if she slips back through her stall and out . . . well, this could be a mighty short visit."

"No need to rush," Ryan said. "I'm quite content to stand and watch."

Once Sam returned to stand beside him, she put aside her worry. Ryan wasn't comparing River Bend with Gold Dust Ranch. Ryan loved horses—hers, his, anyone's. That made him fun to talk with, and Sam found it easy to ignore Rachel, who was standing in the shade of the barn, complaining about the heat.

"I'd love to see that other mustang, the albino," Ryan said when Sam returned.

He pronounced it *al-bee-no*. Sam was wondering why as she showed him toward the ten-acre corral, when there was a sudden commotion from the barn.

No, no, no!

The mare and foal were loose!

Sam was running, arms waving, as Sunny burst from the dark barn with Tempest tucked against her side. For an instant, Sunny was dazzled by the sunlight. While the buckskin's hooves stuttered, Sam rushed toward her. Now, while the mare was disoriented by the open ranch yard and strangers, was her only chance.

Sam slowed her steps, watching Sunny. From the corner of her eye, she caught Ryan moving in the opposite direction. One of them should be able to snag the mare's green halter and slow her down.

"I was almost trampled!" Rachel shrieked.

The scream acted like the siren had on the night of the fire. Then, the high-pitched sound had sent Sunny galloping toward the cattle guard, fleeing for the safety of the open range.

The mare bolted, but Sam stood her ground.

"Sunny, stop. Sunny . . ."

Legs braced, Sam waited for the mare to slide to a stop. In the moment the buckskin's eyes rolled, showing only white, Sam knew she wouldn't.

A half ton of horse struck Sam's shoulder, spinning her all the way around before she fell. The back of her head struck the ground. Her teeth cracked together. Sam had a sudden memory of a skull she'd held in science class. She imagined the little fissures running over the skull. She was pretty sure hers were chattering against each other from the impact.

She'd bitten her tongue, too. Her mouth was filled with blood and that was what made her jump, coughing, to her feet.

"Let's go after them," Ryan said. His car keys jingled in his hand.

"No. Don't want to panic them," Sam said, but her words were garbled. Feeling embarrassed, she spat blood and shuddered. "They might come back, but I can't figure out . . ."

Sam stared toward the barn.

"I closed those bolts and double-checked them. You were here when I did it, right? So how did Sunny get out?"

Rachel lifted her blue suede bag higher on her shoulder. She tucked a wave of dark hair behind one ear.

"Since there's nothing to see," Rachel said, "may we go now, Ryan."

It wasn't a question.

Sam told herself she was being paranoid. No matter how self-centered she was, Rachel wouldn't purposely put Sunny and her new baby in danger.

And Tempest was in terrible danger. Sam couldn't stop thinking of the smoke and fire on that other night. Her heart had nearly stopped as Sunny swooped past the front bumper of the fire engine, and as the mare had passed all the other fleeing horses, she'd been certain the buckskin was never coming back.

If she ran like that now, she could leave Tempest behind. The foal would be vulnerable to weather, predators, cars . . .

"You stupid girl." Ryan pronounced the words in a wondering tone. "You turned them loose."

Sam stared at the siblings. Standing face-to-face, glaring, they might have been mirror images until Rachel lifted her chin.

Then she shrugged.

"They'll have a nice little walk," she said, then gestured toward Sam. "She'll lasso them up, or whatever, and we'll be on our way to the mall."

"Did it ever occur to you—" Ryan began, but then he shook his head. "No, of course it didn't. Sam, I could not be sorrier. Or more mortified. What may I do to help?"

Sam held her temples, trying to think past Rachel's act. She'd try to understand later.

Now she had to help her horses. And she had to hurry. It had started to rain again, adding more peril to the open country.

The first thing she had to do wouldn't be easy, but it had to be done. She needed Jake.

"Do you have any idea where they're herding the cattle?" Sam asked. She gestured vaguely and noticed how the rain dotted her suntanned arm. "If not, call Mrs. Coley." Sam fished the cell phone from her pocket and handed it to Ryan. "Find out. Go there and tell Jake I need him."

Her mind was spinning so far ahead, it was hard to speak slowly, but Ryan nodded as if he understood.

"What are you talking about?" Rachel held a hand over her head, as if it would keep the downpour from harming her hairstyle. "I know you can't possibly be suggesting . . ."

Rachel's jaw dropped. She stared in the direction

Sam had pointed, toward the Calico Mountains. Sam and Ryan ignored her.

"Jake can track them, if I don't find them first," Sam said, blinking against the raindrops. "But I'm going after them on horseback, now. Just on the off chance . . ."

Sam felt dizzy. Multicolored dots frenzied before her eyes and her pulse pounded in her throat. That collision with Sunny and all her restless nights were catching up with her, but it really didn't matter.

Running wild, searching for a herd she'd left almost a year ago, Sunny could break a leg, or her neck. She could plummet down a muddy canyon trail.

Tempest would just stand there, waiting for her mother to get up.

Sam rubbed her eyes. She couldn't let that happen.

"I'll ride Popcorn," Sam muttered to herself. "If any other horse can find them, it's him. They're both mustangs. They've been pasture pals from the first . . ."

"You're not speaking clearly," Rachel said. "I can't hear you."

"Ryan," Sam said, but her eyes locked on Rachel's with such force, the rich girl took a step back. "I really appreciate your help."

Ryan took Rachel's arm and hurried her toward the Mercedes.

"I'll have Jake here as soon as I can," he said over his shoulder, but his grim smile also thanked Sam for not strangling his stupid sister.

* * *

Popcorn might have been a bloodhound in another life, Sam decided.

As soon as she'd ridden the gelding over the bridge, Sam paused. Raindrops tapped on the brim of her brown Stetson. Should she ride straight ahead and take the trail to the Phantom's hidden valley, or turn right, toward Arroyo Azul and War Drum Flats?

Popcorn swung right and burst into a lope. Milky mane blowing back, he welcomed Sam's weight as it shifted forward.

"That's good enough for me," she said, against the albino's neck, and urged him into a gallop.

More for luck than use, Sam had packed Tempest's little halter along with Sunny's lead rope. She touched her saddlebags as if they held a magic charm.

Surefooted and swift, Popcorn took her to a place she didn't want to remember. In this sandy wash, she'd faced a flash flood and helped Jake when he'd broken his leg. But she loosened her grip on the reins and let Popcorn have his head.

The rain had slackened, and a rainbow arched through storm clouds, but Sam's spirits didn't lift.

Her shoulder ached and her head felt swollen. What lay ahead could be bad. She ordered herself to be ready for the worst.

Lightning brightened the dull, pewter sky. Thunder

rolled and Sam stiffened. This was too much like the other night.

One thousand, two thousand . . .

Sam quit counting. No matter how close the lightning was, no matter how worried she was, she had to find Tempest.

"I've trusted you this far," she told Popcorn.

The mustang took the bit, determined to go on.

When Sam heard a thin, shivering neigh, she knew why.

Chapter Sixteen ⟋

Tempest was safe, but she was also alone.

Playing in a puddle, the black filly stamped, watched the droplets sparkle around her, and looked around forlornly. Her high-pitched whinny was so desolate, it should have attracted predators. It was only luck that Popcorn had heard her first.

Tempest greeted Popcorn and Sam with a joyous whinny, then trotted toward them.

Poor baby. Sam's heart squeezed with an old, painful memory. Just like Tempest, she'd been left behind by her mother.

Sam climbed carefully from Popcorn's back. To keep from spooking the filly, she waited. Tempest kept coming, but her steps meandered across the dirt as she stared past Sam and Popcorn, wide-eyed.

She was probably wondering why Sunny wasn't with them, Sam decided. But the filly kept coming.

Once Sam began petting the puzzled foal, Tempest's legs folded for a nap. At least the filly didn't seem hungry. Sam didn't know what she would do when she was.

Right now, she had another problem.

"How do I get you home, baby?"

Sam had seen Dad carry calves across his saddle. Jake had done the same with Faith, Mrs. Allen's blind foal. But Popcorn was only green broke. He hadn't been ridden often by a single rider. Would he tolerate an extra burden and Tempest's long legs dangling against his shoulders?

Should she take a chance? Sam pictured herself falling with the delicate, long-legged foal.

No way. She'd rather exhaust all of them than risk such an accident. Now she had to explain that to the filly.

"Tempest, I'll help you as much as I can, but you'll have to walk out of this riverbed and a little bit farther," she told the dozing foal.

When Tempest's long lashes remained closed against each other, Sam decided to take advantage of the foal's drowsiness.

Moving as silently as she could, Sam took the soft lead rope from her saddlebags and knotted it loosely around the filly's neck. If something startled Tempest,

Sam would have a chance to keep her under control.

"Time to wake up, Sleeping Beauty," Sam coaxed the filly. "I can't carry you, and it's not safe to stay down here." Sam looked up the slanted banks. A sudden storm could turn this low spot into a channel. "The rain could start up again any time, little girl. A flash flood could carry all three of us away."

It wasn't easy to get the foal up and moving, until Sam pretended to be leading Popcorn away. Tempest scrambled to her feet, then hopped sideways at the touch of the rope on her neck.

When the filly didn't fight against the restraint, Sam figured Tempest had decided it was more important to stay with the other horse.

They'd have to walk nearly five miles to arrive home. Sam remembered every awful step she'd ridden with Jake while his face turned paler and his pant leg redder from blood.

But this walk wouldn't be so bad. If the filly were in the wild, she'd have to follow the herd from one feeding ground to another.

They walked slowly and rested often. Overhead, gray clouds parted to show a bright blue sky.

Before long, the foal squeezed ahead of Popcorn and beside Sam.

She let her hand rest on the foal's soft back and didn't try to stop Tempest when she detoured to splash in puddles.

As she watched the lonely filly, Sam realized how

lucky she'd been to find her. This time Tempest had come to her out of confusion. She associated Sam with Sunny.

But Sam knew she might not be that fortunate again. Right away, she needed to forge the same bond with Tempest that she had with the Phantom.

Sam was on the verge of making a plan when Tempest raised her head to neigh, then stood listening.

When Popcorn joined the foal, neighing even louder, Sam hoped Sunny was nearby. But Popcorn held his head high for only an instant, then plodded on.

Afraid of being left behind, Tempest hurried after the albino.

Surely Dark Sunshine would answer if she heard them. But she didn't. Wondering why didn't make Sam feel better.

She watched for the Phantom, too. If Sunny had gone to join him and the stallion came to Sam, the sight of Tempest should lure the mare back.

But the sun was directly overhead now. Their shadows eddied around their feet. It must be noon. The Phantom's band would have searched out shade and water during this hot part of the day.

Sunny wouldn't have an easy time finding them unless she remembered a hiding place. That seemed unlikely, since it had been fall when Sunny had last run with the mustangs.

No hoofprints. No Sunny. No Phantom. Would Jake have better luck spotting a clue?

Just as the River Bend bridge came into view, Sam heard a car on the highway. As she watched, Mrs. Coley drove into view in Linc Slocum's champagne-colored SUV.

Mrs. Coley stopped while she was about three car lengths away so she wouldn't spook the horses.

Just the same, Tempest didn't trust the big, noisy shape. She darted to Popcorn's other side and leaned so close to the white gelding that only her slender legs were visible.

"I see you found Tempest," Mrs. Coley called through the driver's side window. "Want me to give her a ride the rest of the way?"

As tired and battered as she was, Sam smiled. She liked the idea of loading a River Bend horse into Linc Slocum's car, but it might frighten Tempest.

Sam shook her head. "She's doing okay."

"Is she hungry?" Mrs. Coley asked.

Sam remembered their last conversation about feeding Tempest. Making the black filly a foster foal to Hotspot was an even stronger possibility now.

"Not yet," Sam said.

"I'll go ahead, then," Mrs. Coley said.

She accelerated smoothly and quietly away from them and Sam felt grateful all over again that Mrs. Coley had equal shares of kindness and horse sense.

Sam clucked to Popcorn and led him on.

Once they started over the bridge, she glanced back and gasped. Pain forked through her neck tendons and grabbed her shoulder. Who'd guess a horse as small as Dark Sunshine could inflict such damage?

Stiffly, Sam turned her entire body to look back and make sure the sound of her boots on the planks hadn't upset Tempest. The filly didn't seem to have noticed.

She was still shadowing Popcorn, whose head suddenly jerked high. Her nostrils flared open and closed and her hooves danced in a lighter pace.

"Does this smell like home, little girl?" Sam asked.

As her gaze turned from Tempest, Sam saw Popcorn watching her with analytical blue eyes.

"You look smart, boy," she told him. "Why don't you figure out what we're going to do?"

The gelding stopped.

Sam caught her breath and waited for some kind of a response. Popcorn looked longingly down the river.

"Did you see me head down there under the willows with Sunny the other day? Or did she tell you about it?" Sam rubbed the mustang's neck. "Is that what all your calling back and forth was about?"

Popcorn didn't answer. In fact, she guessed he was bored with the conversation, because he took a long stride toward home, and towed Sam along.

The barn smelled weird, but Tempest didn't care.

Recognizing her stall, the filly bounded away from Sam and Popcorn and past Mrs. Coley, who stood there with a bottle.

Sam knew what Tempest was looking for and knew she wouldn't find it.

"She's not there, baby," Sam said.

Ignoring them all, Tempest stood in the middle of the stall.

She snorted. She stamped one tiny hoof. Then Sam saw inside the filly's pink mouth as she neighed and whinnied. Her cries continued until her throat sounded sore.

Then Tempest's head drooped. She sniffed at the wheat straw, lipped it hopelessly, then noticed Mrs. Coley holding an oversized baby bottle.

Tempest shied away, but not far. Her head twitched up twice as she sniffed loudly.

"I've got a little bit of mare's milk here," Mrs. Coley said, waggling the bottle, and Sam wasn't sure whether she was talking to her or Tempest. "Hotspot was nice enough to make the donation, but I'm afraid that while I was trying to heat it back up to body temperature, it scorched. I hope she'll drink it anyway."

The scent must have seemed familiar. As Mrs. Coley stood still, Tempest sniffed around her and the bottle.

Mrs. Coley didn't coax the foal. She let her explore and spoke quietly to Sam. "Ryan called from my cell phone as soon as they got close enough and told me what was going on."

Mrs. Coley met Sam's eyes with a despairing look. "I don't know when Rachel will grow up. I really don't, but that's not important now.

"Ryan said they found your gram making camp near Black Springs—"

"Oh, good!" Sam wanted to celebrate even more loudly, but she didn't want to chance scaring Tempest.

"Luckily, it wasn't far off the road," Mrs. Coley went on. "So they were able to drive the Mercedes straight to your gram's chuck wagon."

Sam thought about wild Nevada and the pale-blue luxury car. Some places had rough and rutted dirt roads and others had no roads at all. Ryan had clearly cared more about his promise than his father's car.

But if Gram was already ahead of the herd, making camp, when would her message be delivered?

"Jake—" Sam began.

"Should be on his way soon. Your gram was expecting a rider in at lunchtime. She said she'd hand him a sandwich and send him back out on a fresh horse to get Jake. She told Ryan they were moving the stock through a mountain pass and he certainly couldn't take the car up there."

Sam sighed. It could be nightfall by the time Jake got to River Bend. If so, it wouldn't make sense to start searching for Sunny until dawn. Her stomach sucked in as if it would touch her backbone.

Unaware of how any of the human words affected her, Tempest licked the bottle, then snorted.

"She's not too sure, but she is interested." Mrs. Coley's tone went higher. Excited, she handed Sam the bottle. "I'll leave you two alone."

Sam held the bottle in trembling hands. She'd bottle-fed two calves—Buddy and Daisy—but this was different. She'd known the calves would leave her sooner or later. If Tempest survived, she could be Sam's for years.

"Tempest," she called to the foal, then made a smooching sound.

The filly's black ears twitched, but she didn't recognize her name yet.

That simple thought suddenly told Sam what was missing between them. All at once, she knew what she needed to create a strong bond between her and the horse Tempest would become.

A secret name.

Sam's pulse raced. The Phantom's secret name had bound him to her after he'd gone wild, after he'd been abused, after every test of their friendship.

The link was doubly strong because no one except Jake knew the stallion had such a name, and no one could ever guess it.

Tempest licked the nipple on the baby bottle. Her eyes rounded in surprise, then she butted it with her nose.

The filly would grow up to be a smart, strong mare. Sam wanted the same bond with the Tempest that she had with her sire.

"Soon, little girl," Sam told the filly. "I'll think of something perfect for you, very soon."

Chapter Seventeen ☙

Sam couldn't believe there'd been so much milk in the bottle. Judging by the amount smeared on each of them, Tempest hadn't had much to eat.

The foal was splattered with white gumminess. Her eyelashes were coated and so were the little whiskers on her chin. White gobs on her neck and down to the middle of her chest showed how she'd struggled in learning to suck from the bottle.

Sam didn't look much better. Spatters had dried on her arms and face. Her hands were a sticky mess.

Still, the effort had been worthwhile. Tempest was satisfied, and too tired to stand for another moment. With a loud sigh, the filly collapsed into the straw.

Sam watched the tiny rib cage rise and fall under its shiny black hide. She hoped the struggle hadn't used more calories than the foal had swallowed.

"Smells like someone burned dinner," said a low voice from behind Sam.

She turned to see Jake silhouetted in the barn door. The fringed outline of his chinks, buckled over his jeans, showed on his legs, but his face was in shadow.

The short leather chaps proved Jake had jumped right from a horse's back into a truck, though the chink must have been uncomfortable to drive in.

Sam was so glad he'd hurried, she wanted to hug him. Instead, she fought back the urge to tell him this was no time to joke about burned milk.

"So?" Jake said, nodding toward the filly. His face looked suddenly grim, as if he'd drawn sad conclusions about the still-missing Sunny.

"I rode out on Popcorn and *he* found Tempest, but I don't know where Sunny's gone. Did Ryan tell you what happened?"

One corner of Jake's mouth moved as if he were about to grin, but he stopped. "Naw, he made Rachel tell me."

"Good," Sam said. She liked Ryan better because he'd forced his twin to take the blame, but it was a very small revenge, and her eyes wandered back to the foal.

"Jake, I don't think Tempest took much from the

bottle, and Mrs. Coley thinks Hotspot might take her on like a twin, but I—" Sam's voice shivered and she stopped.

Don't be a baby, she told herself.

"Don't even say it," Jake told her, holding up a hand.

"I know, it's just . . . I can't stand the idea of the Phantom's baby on Gold Dust Ranch. Linc is probably the Phantom's worst enemy. He'd probably pick earthquakes or cougars or rodeos over Slocum."

"It probably wouldn't work anyway," Jake said. He rubbed the back of his neck.

Sam knew he wanted her to be quiet, but her words kept tumbling out.

"This isn't how it was supposed to go. I listened to everyone—"

"Hey," Jake interrupted. "Maybe we all shoulda kept our mouths shut. Maybe you got confused and the buckskin just—you know. . . ."

She didn't know. She didn't have a clue what he meant, but she must have looked like she was about to burst into another rambling tirade, because he put both hands on her shoulders.

Not only did that keep Sam quiet, but she felt her eyes fill with tears. She held her eyelids as high as she could so there was no chance they'd accidentally spill. Jake could be counted on to freak out if she cried.

He squinted at her face a minute, then stepped back, hands held up as if to stop a charging bull.

"I'm warning you, Brat, get weepy and you're on your own."

"I'm not *weepy*." Sam held her chin higher. She hated that word. "Maybe I had a little dust in my eyes."

"I'm not buyin' that." He pointed his hand at her like it was a revolver. "Probably didn't mean to, but if you blubber and you're not"—he looked up, trying to think of something heinous—"*bleeding*, I'm outta here."

"Okay!" Sam snapped. "Quit wasting time giving me a list of what annoys you. Let's go find Sunny."

"I'll need a horse."

Sam sighed. "I just rode Popcorn ten miles. All we've got are the two oldest horses on the place."

Sam felt disloyal describing Sweetheart and Amigo that way, but it was true. Neither horse had been ridden much, either, so they weren't in shape for a long search.

"I'll saddle them while you go . . ." Jake gestured vaguely toward her legs.

"Go what?"

"Change."

Sam looked down. Her head and shoulders had throbbed so much, she hadn't noticed that her jeans were ripped from midthigh to her knee.

"Might be out after dark," Jake said. "Could get cold."

"I guess when Sunny ran past me—" Sam began.

"She knocked you down?" Jake's eyes widened, but instead of launching into his usual rant about her safety, he asked, "Do I want to hear about it?"

"No. Definitely not," Sam said, pulling the sides of the rip together. "Unless you want to see the blood you require for, uh, what was it? Blubbering?"

Jake turned his back and walked toward the tack room.

"Better hurry," he said. "We're burnin' daylight."

Sam ran upstairs without whimpering. She even shouted an explanation to Mrs. Coley as she passed.

Burning daylight. Sam sucked in a deep breath and looked at her bedroom clock. It was two o'clock. The sun didn't set until about nine. Jake must not have high hopes they'd find Sunny right away.

She peeled off her dusty, ripped jeans and sucked in her breath as she pulled loose a thread that had stuck to her skinned knee. She should clean it up and she'd probably be sorry she hadn't, but it made no sense to waste time on her silly knee when Tempest was waiting for her mother.

It could have been a lot worse, Sam thought as she pulled open a drawer, grabbed the first jeans her fingers touched, and tugged them on.

She stopped when they hit her knee.

"Ow, ow, ow," she moaned, then strengthened her fingers' grip on her jeans' waistband and kept edging them up.

It really hurt.

Trying to distract herself from the pain, she gazed

out her bedroom window that overlooked the ranch yard, the willows, the river . . .

Her hands dropped from her jeans and rose to cover her mouth. If she screamed, the horses might disappear.

In the shallows of the La Charla, closest to the ranch side of the river, Sunny and the Phantom stood head to tail like old friends, nibbling each other's manes.

One quick yank brought her jeans up. She fastened them. Instead of tugging on her boots, Sam jammed her feet into tennis shoes and double-knotted the laces. She needed to move swiftly and silently. And she really didn't need to trip.

She ran down the stairs, dodged Cougar, and waved to Mrs. Coley. There'd be time to explain later.

Jake had Sweetheart and Amigo tied at the hitching rail. He was leaning back, tightening the cinch on Amigo's saddle.

He dropped it and his hands rested on his hips, reading her expression before she stammered out a word.

"Where?" he asked.

"In the river," Sam said as she unsnapped Sweetheart's lead rope. "On this side of the river." She looped the rope around her waist so Sunny wouldn't notice her carrying it until she got close enough to snap it on her green halter. "Kind of by the willows," she said over her shoulder as she ran toward the barn.

Jake kept up in spite of his clumsy boots.

"Bringin' the foal?" he asked.

Sam stopped. She faced him, trying to tell what he was thinking, but Jake's eyes told her nothing.

"Don't you think I should?" she asked.

"There's no should," Jake said. "You know all three of those horses. Decide."

Sam took a deep breath and exhaled.

"I say Sunny will remember she loves her baby the minute she gets a look at her."

"Let's go," Jake said, giving her a gentle push toward the barn.

Please, please, please let her still be there.

Between them, Sam and Jake got Tempest as far as the bridge. Once she was there, the filly's head lifted, testing the warm breeze off the river.

She took two steps onto the bridge. Sam walked beside her.

"This is where I stop," Jake said.

His low voice was a whisper, but Sam whirled to stare at him.

"This is your rodeo, Brat. You'll do better on your own."

She wanted to yell at him or strangle him or shake him until he couldn't see straight. If she went out there alone and Dark Sunshine disappeared, it would be all her fault.

But Sunny shied at the approach of any human.

Twice the Phantom had treated Jake almost like a challenger.

Yet again, Jake was right.

Before she and Tempest stepped off the bridge to the riverbank, Sam saw the two horses clearly.

The river was blue and choppy around their legs, but the horses looked peaceful. For just a minute, Sam kept her hand over Tempest's muzzle.

"Shh," she told the foal as she watched.

White, muscular, and at least a hand taller than the buckskin mare, the Phantom reached down to give Sunny's black mane a gentle bite before moving his nose along her neck and withers. Finally he rested his head on her back.

Sunny's teeth pulled at the Phantom's mane as if she were grooming him, currying out loose hair. Next, she reached up to nibble his withers. Finally, the buckskin mare tapped her black-shaded nose against him, unable to reach high enough to rest her head on his sleek white back.

Sam felt Tempest's muzzle bob in her hand. The foal's warm breath came fast, then faster. Sam dropped her hand away as Tempest reared up on her hind legs.

Tempest's whinny shattered the river's lull. The two mustangs started apart, splashing, plunging.

Surprised, both horses would return home. The Phantom would run for the wild side of the river, but which home would Dark Sunshine choose?

Without a moment's hesitation, both horses crashed through the water. The stallion ran for his herd, milling on the far bank. Sunny moved toward her foal.

Tempest streaked along the riverbank, legs reaching and stretching, a tiny black shadow of her sire.

What if Sunny was only coming back for Tempest, only gathering her up to follow the mighty stallion across the river, to the range?

Sam's heart hammered and her arms curled around her ribs.

For a few moments, mother and foal touched noses. The buckskin whuffled her lips over Tempest's fluffy mane.

The Phantom had reached the opposite shore. He shook and a rainstorm of his own making spun around him, turning drops of river water into rainbow jewels.

Sam swallowed hard. How could the mare not go with him, not join the wild band moving, even now, toward the mountains?

But the buckskin was hesitating, moving around Tempest in aimless circles. Sam had to help her decide.

She walked down the riverbank with the same swinging stride she used when she approached the mare in the pasture.

"Sunny!" Sam called. "Hey, Sunny, what are you thinking? You silly girl. Don't ever leave me behind to feed your baby. I'm really not very good at it. Never again, okay?"

Sunny walked three slow steps toward Sam, then stopped.

The mare gazed across the river.

The wild band of mustangs started up the hillside, led by a honey-colored mare.

Once, before he joined them, the Phantom looked back. A white foreleg struck the shore, before the stallion rose into a rear.

He's Pegasus, Sam thought. Any minute, it seemed, he could vault away from the sand and sagebrush and fly into the blue Nevada sky.

Dark Sunshine shook her head and broke into a trot. She burst past Sam with Tempest close beside her and ran toward River Bend Ranch.

Sunny clopped over the wooden bridge and shied as she spotted Jake on the front porch, giving Sam a smiling, forceful thumbs-up.

But the buckskin ran on, ignoring the neighs from the tethered horses and Popcorn in the ten-acre pasture, to find her way into the barn.

"I cannot believe this," Sam said to herself as she followed. "She's going home, and this is really it."

Sam stepped through the barn door, then paused to catch her breath.

The air inside was hot and stuffy and still smelled like burned milk, but Sam was happy to be there.

Inside the open box stall, Dark Sunshine nursed

her filly, but not for long. It was a greeting, more than a meal, Sam decided as the horses milled around, sniffing the wheat grass straw.

Slowly, quietly, Sam moved to shut the stall door.

She closed herself inside with the horses and waited while Sunny nibbled her sleeve.

"Glad to see me, girl?"

The mare snorted.

"That's good enough for me," Sam said. "But I have something special for your baby."

For a minute, Sam held her breath. Outside, Popcorn gave another yearning whinny. Inside, pigeons fluttered on the rafters. It was time.

She bent from the waist, placed a gentle hand on Tempest's neck, and whispered into her ear.

The night-black filly shivered once. Then, as Sam repeated the word a second time, she stood still and calm. A third and final time, Sam told her the word. Nodding her head, Tempest broke free of Sam and reared on her slim hind legs, glorying in a secret name no one else would ever know.

From

Phantom Stallion
❧ 13 ❧
HEARTBREAK BRONCO

As Sam watched, the wild horses melted into a gully thick with pinion. One horse stayed behind. It was the Phantom.

Sam felt as if a bird fluttered where her heart belonged. Once the Phantom had been hers and she'd seen him every day. Now, each sighting was a gift, a reward for living in this wild country.

"Looks like he's in prime condition," Jake said.

Sam didn't take her eyes from the stallion. Still, she smiled. Sometimes it seemed as if Jake and the Phantom were enemies, but, like dad, Jake was a horseman as well as a cattleman. He had to admire the splendid stallion.

"He's not paying much attention to Jinx," Sam said. "I can't figure that out."

The Phantom waited, lips lowered near the ground.

"He's watching," Jake said, amused. "He's pretending to graze, but he's luring the gelding close enough to get a good look."

Jake was right.

If the Phantom believed Jinx was set on stealing

mares, he would have flexed his neck muscles in challenge.

Instead, the silver stallion moved with trancelike steps, acting as if he sought nothing more than a tender bite of grass.

"Do you think Jinx is fooled?" Sam asked.

Neck drawn back, ears pointed toward the Phantom, Jinx didn't look submissive. He continued toward the trampled area around the pond.

Would the Phantom let him drink?

"We'd better stop," Jake said, braking until the pick-up halted. "If they think the truck's a threat, the stallion might let Jinx join the herd until danger's passed. My dad said he's seen two stallions do that — join forces against an enemy, sort of."

Sam wasn't so sure. The Phantom was always looking for trouble and she'd seen him fight other stallions. The battles had been vicious and bloody. She couldn't believe he'd let another male mingle with his mares.

"Watch out," she blurted as the Phantom raised his head, flattened his ears, then lunged, mouth open.

Jinx stopped, though the pale stallion had only advanced a few feet closer.

"I think," Sam said quietly, "He's just telling Jinx who's the boss around here."

"Maybe," Jake said.

Mane glinting like tinsel, the Phantom trotted forward.

Jinx looked away, swishing his black tail in apparent boredom, though Sam would bet he was still watching the stallion from the corner of his eye.

Why didn't Jinx retreat? That's all it would take to satisfy the stallion.

When Jinx held his ground, the Phantom lowered his head into a herding position. His shoulder muscles bunched as he advanced. The gelding sidestepped, eyes rolling.

Suddenly aware that Jake was rummaging around in the truck, Sam pried her gaze from the horses.

"What are you doing?" she asked.

"Getting out. Your horse is gonna drive that gelding back this way. When he does, I'll rope him."

"I'm coming with you," Sam said, but the truck door had just closed when the Phantom charged.

It turned out Jake was wrong. Instead of coming toward them, Jinx ran after the mares. They'd passed through the gully. Now they stood on the ridge line, switching their tails as they gazed down at the excitement below.

A short neigh of rage burst from the Phantom, as he lunged after the gelding.

Hearing the stallion's hooves closing on him, Jinx increased his speed.

"He can run," Jake said.

Gusts of wind might have blown at his heels, keeping him a half length ahead of the Phantom.

A stranger would have taken Jinx for the horse who'd spent winter in the wild. His grulla coat was dull and patchy, his movements rough.

The silver stallion shone in the sun. Living off the land, searching out each mouthful of food had made him sleek, lean and strong. He moved with a tireless grace.

Still, Sam admitted, each time the Phantom put on a burst of speed, Jinx surged ahead.

"Why would a man give away a horse that can run like that?" Jake asked.

"I can't believe it," she whispered. "The Phantom's got to catch him."

Jinx no longer chased after the mares. He flew across the playa, wheeling right when the Phantom tried to nip his neck. Then he rushed left when the frustrated stallion circled to the other side, trying to ram his mighty shoulder against the gelding's, to shove him off balance.

Branches cracked as the horses trampled a clump of sagebrush in their path. The herbal smell blew to Sam on a hot wind.

"When are they going to stop?" she asked.

"It's a grudge match, now, but the gelding didn't drink," Jake pointed out. "He'll slow down soon."

And then what? Sam wondered.

Even though they were still a half mile away, she heard the horses' breathing. Their speed said they weren't exhausted, but they were working hard.

Which horse would win? A tangle of loyalty and sympathy wouldn't let Sam take sides.

And then, she didn't have to.

Through a secret set of signals, the horses agreed to stop. Half-rearing, the Phantom rose above the gelding, pawing with his front hooves. He didn't touch the grulla, but he left no question about his dominance.

Jinx backed toward the pond, watching the stallion return to all fours. He stared after the Phantom as the pale horse trotted to his herd.

"Wow." Sam felt air whoosh through her lips as if she'd been holding her breath.

Beside her, Jake tightened his grip on the coiled rope in his left hand. He turned his right hand, rolling his wrist, loosening it up for a throw. As he took a step toward the horse, he gave Sam a look that said stay back.

She didn't argue. Jinx wasn't acting too spooked now, but he'd proven he'd be tough to catch if he decided to run. It only made sense for her to stay at the truck, blending in, while Jake roped him.

Jake held the lariat against his leg as he sauntered toward the pond. If the horse had ever been roped before, he wouldn't be fooled.

The grulla drank noisily. In the instant he raised his dripping muzzle, Jake sent a loop to settle gently over the horse's head.

Jinx snorted and Jake stood still as the horse

backed splashing into the pond. When he reached the end of it, the rope tightened about halfway down the grulla's neck, pressing a flat spot in his Mohawk mane.

Jake made a clucking noise. The gelding released a sigh that shook his entire body and then, when Jake turned to walk back toward the trailer, he followed.

Read all the Phantom Stallion books!

AVON BOOKS
An Imprint of HarperCollins*Publishers*
www.harperteen.com